"Ignoring the attraction is only making it worse."

The memory of what it felt like to be in his arms roared through her. The seductive answer to her question seemed impossible to ignore when he stood so close to her, more appealing than any man she'd ever met.

"At least we agree on what's not working," she murmured.

"Why don't you let me make you my priority for the rest of the day, Miranda?" Kai suggested, reaching out to skim a knuckle along her cheek.

Being with him would be so much more complicated than that. But when was the last time she'd put what she'd wanted ahead of everything else?

Opening her eyes, she found his.

"Yes. I want to do more than see a room with a bed. I want to be in one. With you."

And then, all at once, both hands cupped her face, lifting her chin for his kiss.

* * *

Her Texas Renegade by Joanne Rock is part of the Texas Cattleman's Club: Inheritance series.

D0360756

Dear Reader,

It's always a thrill to return to Royal, Texas, where passions run high and romance is around every corner. I found so much to admire about Miranda Dupree, a heroine who has been misjudged by the world and disappointed by her marriage. Underneath all her fierce ambition, she has a huge heart.

And that's something she needs to protect around tech wizard Kai Maddox! Just when she thought no one could ever tempt her to love again, she's faced with the man who broke her heart—and maybe the *only* man who stands a chance of fixing it.

I hope you'll enjoy the conclusion to the Texas Cattleman's Club: Inheritance series, and please don't forget to visit me at joannerock.com to find out when my Dynasties: Mesa Falls series continues in Harlequin Desire!

Happy reading,

Joanne Rock

JOANNE ROCK

HER TEXAS RENEGADE

Special thanks and acknowledgment are given to Joanne Rock for her contribution to the Texas Cattleman's Club: Inheritance miniseries.

HARLEQUIN®
DESIRE™

Recycling programs for this product may not exist in your area.

ISBN-13: 978-1-335-20908-5

Her Texas Renegade

Harlequin Enterprises ULC
22 Adelaide St. West, 40th Floor
Toronto, Ontario M5H 4E3, Canada
www.Harlequin.com

Printed in U.S.A.

Joanne Rock credits her decision to write romance after a book she picked up during a flight delay engrossed her so thoroughly that she didn't mind at all when her flight was delayed two more times. Giving her readers the chance to escape into another world has motivated her to write over eighty books for a variety of Harlequin series.

Books by Joanne Rock

Harlequin Desire

Dynasties: Mesa Falls

The Rebel
The Rival
Rule Breaker
Heartbreaker

Texas Cattleman's Club: Inheritance

Her Texas Renegade

Visit her Author Profile page at Harlequin.com, or joannerock.com, for more titles.

You can also find Joanne Rock on Facebook, along with other Harlequin Desire authors, at Facebook.com/harlequindesireauthors!

For Marcie Robinson,
whose books I can't wait to read.

Prologue

Five months ago

Miranda Dupree Blackwood took deep breaths before the meeting with her ex-stepchildren where they would learn the contents of Buckley Blackwood's last will and testament. Miranda had flown from her home in New York City to Royal, Texas, because of Buck's highly unorthodox last wishes. Knowing what her wily ex-husband had planned for today made her ill, but she understood the role he wanted her to play, and she wasn't going to turn her back on it.

"Are you sure you want to be there for this?" Kace LeBlanc, Buckley's lawyer, asked her as the hour drew near for the meeting that she imagined would be like facing a firing squad. "You don't have to attend in person."

Miranda was upstairs in her former marital home, Blackwood Hollow, where she was trying to make herself comfortable again after a three-year absence. Kace had been kind to stop by early to check in with her. She'd received the attorney in the upstairs den, the space she'd used as her office during her marriage to the wealthy finance mogul. So much had changed since she'd left Royal after her divorce. One thing that remained the same, however, was the animosity of her adult stepchildren, who would soon hate her more than ever once they understood the terms of their father's will.

"I'm committed," she assured herself as much as Kace, knowing that behind Buckley's unconventional strategy, his heart had been in the right place when he set up his terms. "I just wish he didn't have to be so damned secretive about his motives."

Kace shook his head, pacing in front of one of the windows overlooking the front gates of the sprawling ranch estate. "I urged him to make peace with his kids before his death, but he insisted this was the only way. You know how tough it was to argue with him."

How well she remembered. Miranda hugged herself tighter, bracing for the role she would have to play over the next few months until Buck's real motives made themselves apparent.

She'd had zero interaction with the Blackwood family since leaving Royal. Which, no doubt, was how of all three of Buck's grown children preferred it. Their combined venom toward Miranda for marrying their wealthy father in the first place hadn't subsided, not even when she left the marriage behind without taking anything of the Blackwood estate with her. She'd walked away with the same assets that she'd entered into the union, thanks to an ironclad prenup that they'd both wanted. Miranda did just fine for herself, and she preferred it that way.

"It's going to be a rough few months," she murmured, seeing a glint through the front window and guessing that the guests were already starting to arrive for the meeting. "I'll do my best to support Buckley's wishes, but you know there may be an uprising in the office once you tell them what the will says."

"I'm aware," Kace told her grimly, turning away from the window. "Just remember that Buckley believed in you. He saw what you were doing with Goddess and he was impressed. He knew you'd be a good steward for his estate until his kids are ready to take over."

She nodded, taking some comfort from that, at least. If only the family knew that they would receive their inheritances eventually. That one day, Miranda would hand everything back to the Blackwoods once each of his children was more settled. From the bank to the house, none of it would remain hers, although Buckley had donated an incredibly generous sum to her charity, Girl to the Nth Power, for her time and trouble in overseeing the distribution of his estate. She was humbled by the trust he'd placed in her, even if she hated that he was being so secretive with his true heirs.

Buckley may not have been the best husband, but he'd always supported her efforts to build her own business and their split had been amicable. Without his encouragement, she might not have driven her Goddess line of health and lifestyle centers into the level of nationwide success they now experienced. She'd pushed her way onto the *Forbes* list last year.

Now that she would be staying in Royal for at least the next several months, she had told her producer she couldn't be in New York when filming started for a new season of *Secret Lives of NYC Ex-Wives*, a reality show that had spurred the Goddess brand to huge new heights.

But Nigel had told her not to worry. She had a feeling he was making plans to film the show down here if he could talk her castmates into making the move. Which would bring a whole other level of chaos to an already complicated time in her life.

Still, she was going to forge ahead. First she just needed to get through today. Buckley Blackwood was about to deliver a devastating blow to his offspring, robbing them of everything he'd promised since they were children.

A cold sweat dotted Miranda's head. Buckley's

children had called her the "step-witch" when she'd joined the family. What would they think of her today when they learned their father had left every shred of their inheritance to her?

One

Present Day

Miranda had hoped today's brunch could be a girls-only affair for her friends from the *Secret Lives of NYC Ex-Wives* show, but producer Nigel Townshend had convinced her he needed some footage at a more intimate gathering. Since the show had started filming in Royal, Texas, thanks to Miranda being tied to the town, their schedule had been packed with big, glitzy parties.

Especially engagement parties. Romance seemed to be in the air in Royal. Her stepson Kellan was now married with a baby on the way. Kellan's sister, Sophie, had married Miranda's producer, Nigel, just a few weeks ago. Their brother Vaughn had just gotten engaged, as had two of Miranda's castmates. And Darius Taylor-Pratt, her new business associate, had managed to find love, too—after he'd come to town to learn the stunning news that he was Buck's illegitimate son. The discovery had been a shock, but the love he'd found—or rather, rediscovered—with his former sweetheart, Audra, had softened the blow.

Weddings were all anyone wanted to discuss anymore. Even now, Miranda's castmate Lulu Shepard used the time as an opportunity to discuss plans for her nuptials to Kace LeBlanc, Buckley's lawyer.

"Do you have a venue in mind for the wedding, Lu?" Miranda asked her newly engaged costar.

They were seated at a table under the extended eaves that shaded the outdoor entertaining area near the guesthouse pool at Blackwood Hollow. In the five months that Miranda had spent in Royal since the reading of the will, she'd come to feel even more at home here than she had during her marriage to Buckley. Now that she and Kace had told the siblings about how their father had actually chosen to divide up his estate, her work here was almost done. That was why she was staying in the guesthouse at the ranch—the property belonged to Kellan and his wife now. She'd been surprised and touched when he'd invited her to stay in the guesthouse for as long as she needed while she wrapped things up in Royal. Her real inheritance had been the opportunity to mend

her relationships with the Blackwood heirs, something she'd genuinely enjoyed.

Even if it involved enough weddings and engage-
ments to make the most reluctant romantic a little
envious.

"You *have* to marry in New York," Rafaela Marchesi announced, flipping dark, cascading waves
over one shoulder to ensure her good side was visible to the camera. A five-time divorcee on the hunt
for husband number six, Rafaela thrived on trouble-
making and she played the diva for all it was worth.
"Bring the party back where we belong."

Henry the cameraman lingered on the resident
diva while Sam swiveled his second camera for a
reaction shot from Lulu.

"No." Lulu tilted her champagne glass in Rafaela's
direction, pointing it at her and showing off her amaze-
balls new diamond at the same time. "We're getting
married in Royal, that much I know."

"Good," Miranda interjected, not wanting the
brunch to turn into a snipe-fest. Audiences might
love that kind of thing, but Miranda wouldn't let popular demand turn Lulu's wedding preparations into
nonstop bickering. "It's only fitting to celebrate here
when it all began in Royal for you two lovebirds."

Never let it be said Miranda didn't have a soft side,
even if romance hadn't worked out well for her. She
and Buckley had split on friendly enough terms, but
the dissolution of her marriage still felt like a failure

on her part. And lately, her thoughts were full of the man who'd held her heart before Buck.

Kai Maddox, the cybersecurity expert she needed to review the digital encryption measures at Blackwood Bank. No doubt that's why her long-ago lover had taken up residence in her brain this week after years of doing her best to forget him. Well, that and the fact that they'd shared a searing kiss the first time she'd asked for his professional help—right before he'd refused her outright. She'd have to swallow her pride and try asking him again. He might have a sketchy past, but no one could argue the man excelled at his job. Besides, his new company, Madtec, was local, based in nearby Deer Springs, where he'd grown up.

"Cheers to being a Texas bride, Lu." Zooey Kostas, the youngest one of the ex-wives at thirty years old, lifted her glass to toast their friend, her diamond-encrusted bangles sliding down her slender wrist. Her honey-colored hair and green eyes gave her a fresh-faced appeal in spite of her hard-partying ways. "I want you to get married here anyway."

The five women at the table, including Seraphina "Fee" Martinez, who was also due to marry a local, lifted their glasses automatically to toast the bride. Miranda sipped her mimosa, savoring the fresh-squeezed oranges even more than the champagne, while Rafaela rolled her eyes.

"Zooey, darling, you've lost your mind," Rafaela declared, leaning in and piling on the drama for a good sound bite. "Why should we waste ourselves on cowboys in the Lone Star State when we can have our pick of Wall Street billionaires in Manhattan?"

Miranda slouched in her seat, so done with Rafaela Marchesi. Was this what her life had amounted to, trading barbs with frenemies over cocktails?

Lulu looked ready to fire off a comeback, but Zooey surprised them all with a wicked laugh that bordered on a cackle.

"Waste ourselves? You're just jealous you haven't bagged a rich Texan the way Lulu and Fee have." Zooey tossed her napkin on the table and then stood, her cream-colored halter pantsuit draping beautifully as she moved. "Excuse me, ladies, but I've lost my appetite."

The sudden diva-exit was so un-Zooey-like that Miranda and Lulu turned to one another at the same time, with Lulu looking as shocked as Miranda felt.

"Bitch," Rafaela muttered, studying her manicure. "Clearly, she's not getting laid enough if she's acting like such a shrew."

Miranda smothered a laugh while Lulu went back to brainstorming good places to exchange vows with Kace. No doubt the production team had filmed all the footage they needed for this week's episode anyway. And since the show had plenty of juicy moments for viewers, maybe Miranda stood a chance of sneaking away from the camera crew and Blackwood Hollow for the afternoon.

She needed to meet with Kai Maddox sooner

rather than later to convince him to take on Black-wood Bank as a client, even though thinking about another confrontation with her former flame tied her in knots. What had she been thinking to allow that damned kiss to happen in the first place? Kai was the only man to ever shred her restraint so thoroughly.

Now that Vaughn knew he'd inherited the bank, it was time to pass everything over to him officially—but first, she needed someone to check into the ir-regularities she'd noticed while going over the books. She owed it to Buckley's family to pass over the reins of the company in good standing, especially now that she was only just starting to form real relationships with them. But she had no intention of letting her television audience see her fork up a bite of humble pie with her sexy-as-sin ex-lover to ask for his help.

Again.

He'd practically thrown her out on the street the last time she'd approached him. Right after the kiss that set her on fire every time she remembered it. Things were going to be complicated with Kai.

Assuming she even made it past the front door of Madtec.

This time, she'd simply have to make him an offer he couldn't refuse.

Kai Maddox strode across the rooftop terrace of Madtec's recently built headquarters in Deer Springs, lingering near the half wall and glass partition that overlooked the parking area as his afternoon meeting broke up. A light breeze blew from the west, but it did little to cool the afternoon heat. Soon, the days would be too warm for terrace meetings, but Kai planned to take advantage of the outdoor spot for as long as he could, knowing the benefit of fresh air and green space. He'd learned to make his health and mental wellness a priority since his teen years when he'd all but fallen into his computer screen, spending every waking moment honing his skills as a coder, a developer and, yes—occasionally—as a hacker.

Nothing prepared a coder for building the best digital encryption quite as well as breaking down someone else's.

Madtec had moved into its Deer Springs location shortly after the new year, as soon as work crews had finished the custom-designed, high-tech office building. With five floors and the rooftop terrace, it was more square footage than the Maddox brothers currently needed for their growing tech business, but the cost of real estate here was reasonable and Kai had faith that Madtec would only grow.

Even if he didn't return Miranda Dupree's phone calls. He was doing just fine without taking business from a woman who'd dumped him the moment someone richer came along.

"Did you need anything else, Kai?" his personal assistant called to him from the steel-beam pavilion in the middle of the rooftop as he packed up his notes and tablet. Amad was new to the job, but the guy was efficient and eager to learn.

"No, thank you. I've got a meeting with Dane soon, but first I'm going to review the data penetration tests again." Kai and his brother, Dane, had new fraud-protection software almost ready to take to market, but first he'd asked his old hacking buddies to try to crack it.

So far, the issues in the software they'd uncovered had been minor, but he wanted to ask for one more opinion. He refused to rush the product to market without thorough testing.

"Sure thing, boss." Amad jammed everything in a leather binder and headed for the door leading back into the building, but he paused to look down at his phone before opening it. "The main desk says you have someone here to see you. Miranda Dupree? She's not on your schedule."

He cursed silently.

Miranda had cornered him at his hotel in New York last month and things had spiraled out of control fast. How he'd ended up kissing her was still a mystery to him, but that's just what had happened, even though he'd spent ten years hating her.

As much as he would have preferred to ignore her forever in light of their nasty breakup a decade ago, Kai suspected the knee-jerk reaction would be too damned self-indulgent. Bad enough that he'd been ignoring her calls. Now that she'd shown up in person, sending her away would be too visible, and might reflect badly on the company. She was a respected businesswoman. She'd made the *Forbes*

list. He would at least do her the courtesy of a meeting before he refused whatever the hell she wanted
from him.

"I'll meet her in my office," he said, deciding the
quickest way to end this would be face-to-face—and
one-on-one. He sure as hell didn't want anyone else
around to see the chemistry that still sparked between them. "You can send her up in five."

"Will do." Amad shoved his phone in his pocket
before he left the rooftop.

Kai followed him down to the penthouse office
a few moments later. He shared the top floor with
Dane, the two copresident suites separated by an
executive conference room. Both Maddox brothers
had private terraces on opposite sides of the building.
On a clear day, Kai could see the roof of the humble
house where he'd grown up.

There were a lot of unhappy memories in Deer
Springs, but some good ones, too—and the hope for
more in the future. Madtec had brought hundreds
of jobs to the community that had shaped him, and
that gave him a lot of satisfaction. Far more than he
was going to get from this meeting with Miranda.

By the time Kai arrived in his office through the
private back entrance, Amad was just opening the
double doors to admit his guest in the front.

And damn, but she still had a potent effect on him.

Her fiery-red hair was cut just above her shoulders, with her curls tamed so that her hair swooped
over one eye. She was dressed in a fitted black suit

that showed off her figure—although not quite as much as the strapless red dress he'd seen her in last time. That dress had been... Damn.

Fantasy worthy. He was grateful to today's suit for covering more of her. She remained toned and athletic thanks to her lifelong commitment to yoga, and she had the lean limbs of a dancer. But her generous curves were more the pinup variety, giving her a silhouette that made men of all ages stop and stare. Including him, damn it.

He forced his gaze to her ice-blue eyes.

"Hello, Kai. Thank you for seeing me on such short notice." She smiled warmly at Amad before Kai's assistant left the room.

"You didn't leave me much choice," he informed her shortly, gesturing to one of the two wingbacks in front of his desk. "Please, have a seat."

She disregarded the offer, remaining on her feet as he did. Even in heels she was half a foot shorter than him, but her cool demeanor still commanded attention and exuded authority along with her smoking-hot sexiness.

She'd gained confidence along with over-the-top wealth from her marriage to Buckley Blackwood. Besides a national fitness empire and popular television series, he was certain that Miranda had access to a level of financial support that Kai had to wrestle and scrabble for from investors. The Blackwood name had unlocked a whole world for her. Kai's courtship, on the other hand, had consisted mostly of diner dates and motorcycle rides whenever he'd had a free moment from the endless stream of work that had claimed most of his time.

"You could have ignored me, the way you've snubbed my phone messages." She peered around the office.

He'd purposely kept it clutter-free and impersonal, a mostly soundproof haven for him to think. The walls were all gray stone except for the windows behind the desk. Lights ringed the tray ceiling, hidden in the molding to mimic the effect of daylight at any hour. His desk was glass-topped with steel underneath. Industrial and functional. He wondered briefly how it looked through her eyes.

If he was being honest, he wondered how *he* looked through her eyes, too. Ten years ago, he'd been knee-deep with the old hacker crowd, and skirting the law as he unraveled the most complex facets of data encryption. Miranda had been older than him, with a drive and ambition he admired and an ease with her sensuality that he'd found sexy as hell.

But she'd turned her back on him the moment she met Buckley Blackwood and his millions. And he wasn't about to take a trip down memory lane with her, even if memories of that rogue kiss in New York had put her in his thoughts all too often lately.

"Deer Springs is a small town, Miranda." He rounded the desk to stand closer to her, noting the way her eyes followed him. "I wasn't about to feed the local rumor mill with stories about me refusing to see the town's most illustrious native."

She laughed but it was a brittle sound. "Please. Deer Springs is practically Silicon Valley compared to Sauder Falls."

He'd forgotten she was technically from the next town over, a fact never referenced in her bio since Sauder Falls was a dingier town that had never recovered from a mill closing many years prior. When they'd met, Miranda had been working part-time at a diner in Deer Springs while she ran a local yoga studio and gave classes at another fitness center in Royal. Her big dreams and hard work to achieve them had captivated him since he understood that thirst to do something more.

"Nevertheless, your name is well-known around here." He was close enough to her to catch a hint of her fragrance, the same scent that made him think of night-blooming flowers. The sooner he sent her on her way, the better. There wouldn't be any surprise kisses this time. "And now that you've got your audience, what is it you want from me? I thought I made it clear I wasn't interested in doing business with you the last time we met."

Her lips compressed into a thin line at the reminder of their last meeting. After the kiss that had been so damned unexpected, he'd recovered by assuring her he wouldn't so much as cross the street for her anymore. Harsh? Not considering the way she'd dumped him.

No sense pretending they had much to say to one another anymore.

"I'm temporarily managing Blackwood Bank," she began, coming straight to the point as she tilted her chin. "And I need to update the security before I pass over the reins to the Blackwood heirs. You wouldn't be doing business with me so much as with the Blackwoods."

Surprise registered. He'd thought maybe she wanted help with Goddess, her line of fitness studios. Blackwood Bank was a client of a whole different caliber. Encryption for a financial institution was extremely complex. It might have been tempting, if not for the woman who made the offer.

She was tempting, too. But in all the wrong ways when he needed to focus on his business.

"But as you pointed out, you're managing the bank right now. You honestly expect me to work for you?" Folding his arms, he leaned against his desk. Waiting. Willing his thoughts to stay on business and his boots to stay firmly planted.

No touching. No thinking about touching.

Even though the pulse at the base of her throat leaped frantically, drawing his eye and making him wonder what would happen if he ran his tongue over that very place. He'd be willing to bet she'd burst into flames. But then, he would too, and he'd be damned if that happened.

"Not for *me*. For the bank." Opening her purse, she removed a manila folder and placed it on his desk. The movement put her body in dangerously enticing proximity to his. "I have a contract ready, but if the terms aren't to your liking—"

"No." He didn't need to look at the terms.

"No?" She left the folder on the desk and her blue eyes met his. "Kai, this is a very good offer. The bank deserves the kind of data protection your company specializes in, and since you're local—"

"Madtec is busy." He was being abrupt. Borderline unprofessional. But he didn't like the way she affected him and didn't intend to tempt fate by spending any more time together than was absolutely necessary.

She gripped the leather of her designer purse tighter, her short nails and simple French manicure oddly reminding him she wasn't quite as high maintenance as the other women on her reality television show. There was still something more down-to-earth about Miranda.

Not that he'd ever watched more than a two-minute clip.

"I understand," she told him finally, inclining her head with the grace of a medieval queen. "But I'll leave the contract here and hope you'll reconsider. Perhaps Dane would feel differently."

Dane would kick his ass for turning down a client like Blackwood Bank. But Kai said nothing.

Realizing he was probably staring her down like a street thug, Kai shook off the frustration and straightened.

"Thank you for thinking of us," he said with too

much formality, ready to get back to his work. "My assistant can show you out."

Not that Miranda Dupree had ever needed help walking away.

"I could assign someone else to be the point person for the bank." She tossed out the compromise, clearly sensing he wasn't going to budge. "You'd never have to see me once you agreed to the job."

He wasn't about to let her see that the offer had appeal. He managed a cool smile. "Afraid you'd end up in my bed again if we worked together, Miranda?"

"Not at all." She folded her arms and peered up at him like she knew exactly what he was thinking. "Are you, Kai?"

She let the question hang between them for a long moment before she turned on her heel and walked out of his office with the same quiet confidence that had accompanied her through the doors in the first place. Kai didn't breathe again until she was out of sight. And hell, he couldn't help but wonder if she had a point. Because she still tempted him like no woman he'd ever known.

Even if he couldn't trust her.

Shoving aside the contract she'd left behind, he pulled out his laptop from a hidden drawer in one gray stone wall, and got to work.

Humble pie tasted even worse when choked down with no results.

Miranda fumed on her way out of the Madtec offices, thoroughly irritated with herself for wasting time driving to Deer Springs only to have Kai Maddox reject her offer without even stirring himself to look at it. He'd been more concerned with making sure she knew how easily he could ignite the old attraction between them.

And she couldn't very well dispute it. The heat rolled off him in waves, melting her defenses like they'd never been there in the first place.

She took the stairs—she preferred stairs whenever possible to up her steps, especially when there was anger to be stomped out—and was surprised to discover the Madtec stairwell seemed to be designed for employee wellness. Motivational phrases were painted on the walls, and the stairs were wide enough to accommodate several people at once. There was even a "runners' lane" painted in red to one side. With vinyl walls and ventilation fans, the staircase implemented some of the same techniques she used in her fitness centers to keep the space clean and well aired.

And how frustrating was it to find something to admire about Kai when she wanted to stay furious with him?

"Ms. Dupree?" A young woman with a swinging ponytail yanked her earbuds free as she locked eyes with Miranda and halted on her way up the steps. "I love your show so much. Is it true the *Secret Lives of NYC Ex-Wives* is leaving Royal soon? It's been so fun seeing sites close to home on TV."

"Thank you." Miranda smiled warmly, knowing the importance of connecting positively with viewers who invested their time in the program. "We will be filming in Royal for at least a few more weeks," assuming Lulu and the show's production team could pull together a big wedding in time, "but next season we'll be returning to New York."

"We'll really miss you," the woman said sincerely, digging in her messenger bag and pulling out a pen and paper. "Especially since you grew up around here and have ties to the area. May I have an autograph?"

"Of course." Miranda signed the back of the woman's grocery receipt before they went their separate ways, her thoughts snagging on the fan's words about being native to the region.

Miranda hadn't visited her mother since she'd been back in Texas. Nor had her mother come to Royal to see her, which was even more surprising in light of how thoroughly Virginia "Ginny" Dupree loved Blackwood Hollow. And how hard she'd once lobbied to have a role on *Secret Lives of NYC Ex-Wives*. She'd been angry at Miranda for not giving her that chance. Although not as angry as she'd been at Miranda for leaving her marriage in the first place. It had made her furious that Miranda signed a prenup—and walked away with nothing from Buck.

How stupid can you be? she'd shouted at Miranda over the phone, her diction sloppy from a prescription painkiller addiction that ebbed and flowed according to what was going on in her life at the time.

Breathe in. Breathe out.

Yoga, and all the mindful breathing that went with it, had been helping keep Miranda grounded her entire adult life. The teachings of Goddess centers everywhere weren't just about being physically fit. All that breathing definitely helped her emotional and mental health, too.

By the time she reached the main floor of Madtec, Miranda didn't feel quite as annoyed with Kai. Looking around at the design touches in the building, from the vintage video game posters that decorated the café walls to the courtyards and green spaces that seemed to give employees plenty of options for working outdoors in mild weather, Miranda had to admire the employee-centered corporate environment he'd given his workforce.

Kai Maddox might be a former hacker who'd skirted the law in the years he'd worked to learn the computer security business from the inside out, but there was no denying he'd turned his knowledge into an incredibly successful undertaking. Moreover, he'd given back to his hometown by building his corporate headquarters here. She'd read an article about a community center he'd built close to the diner where she used to work.

Where they'd met.

She wouldn't be driving by that on her way out of town, however. Shoving out the front doors of

Madtec into the late afternoon sunlight, Miranda had enough thoughts of Kai crowding her head for one day. He'd packed on more muscle since they'd dated a decade ago, but there was no mistaking the always-assessing, smoldering green eyes and the scar on his jaw where he'd collided with the road on one of his motorcycle tours. The tattoos she remembered had been covered up by his custom Italian suit, but she found herself remembering every swirl and shadow of the intricate ink.

Stop.

She told herself not to give the reformed bad boy another thought. Clearly, he'd put her in his past and had no intention of spending more time with her than was absolutely necessary, no matter that she'd been prepared to pay him well.

She'd simply have to find someone else to review the Blackwood Bank digital security since Kai was determined not to help her. She'd been a fool to expect anything else. Maybe while she worked on bringing the cybersecurity of the bank up to snuff, she would have firewalls installed on her heart, too.

Two

"What the hell is the matter with you?" Dane Maddox stormed into Kai's office the next afternoon, a stainless-steel mug of coffee in one hand, and a sheaf of papers in the other.

Or, it *was* in the other hand until he slid the packet across Kai's desk.

The contract with the logo from Blackwood Bank emblazoned on the top pinwheeled across the glass surface before a corner lodged under his laptop.

Recognizing there wasn't a snowball's chance in hell of getting any work done until he addressed whatever had his brother fired up, Kai closed his computer and shoved back from the desk to meet Dane's glare. Dane might be two years younger than

Kai, but he had all of Kai's tech smarts and a level of business savvy worthy of someone who'd been in the corporate world for twice as long. Kai was proud of him, even when he was being a pain in the ass.

"Let's see," Kai mused aloud, humoring him. "Depending who you talk to, it could be the chip on my shoulder. Or that I'm too much of a workaholic. And the whole thrill-seeking thing rubs some people the wrong way—"

"I'll tell you what your problem is," Dane continued, jabbing a finger on Kai's desk. "You're too damned bullheaded to recognize *this*—" he jabbed the contract twice more "—is everything we've been waiting for."

Tension bunched up the muscles in his shoulders, twisting its way along his neck.

"Madtec is thriving," Kai reminded him. "There's no need to affiliate ourselves with—" How to phrase his reservations about Miranda? About *himself* when he was around Miranda? "—people we don't care to work with just to make a buck."

Dane paced around Kai's office, his dark brown hair overdue for a cut and giving silent testament to how many hours he'd been putting into the new software testing.

"This contract is not with *people*." Dane loosened his tie a fraction although it wasn't even noon yet. "This is a contract to partner with one of the top ten privately held banks in the country, Kai."

He hardly needed to be reminded. But the knowledge didn't ease the knot in his throat at the thought of seeing more of Miranda. She might be easy on the eyes, but she'd been hell on his heart. Worse, Kai had been so thoroughly distracted by their affair and the thought of losing her that he'd taken his focus away from a project he'd been working on with his brother. The job had required a large-scale "almost" hack, since the first step toward preventing hackers from gaining access to any system is to learn how hacking is done. Quietly breaching a system—with zero malicious intent—had been a delicate task with devastating consequences if it was mishandled, but Kai had let Dane step up his role, confident his brother had the skills to monitor the program while Kai wooed Miranda.

The fact that Dane had done prison time for Kai's mistake would weigh on him forever. But bringing that up now would only tick off his agitated brother even more.

"When we started this company," Kai reminded him instead, "we agreed we would take the work we *wanted*—"

"I'm going to stop you right there." Dane charged toward the desk again to retrieve the paperwork. "When we came up with our mission statement, we agreed to work with companies that shared our values wherever possible, and I stand by that. But that doesn't mean we're suddenly going to turn down the chance to work with a reputable financial institution because an old flame happened to deliver the offer."

His brother laid the sheaf on top of his laptop and placed a heavy silver pen nearby.

"Does this mean you want us to take the project, even when we're already running at full capacity to get the new software to market?"

"We're only running at capacity because we haven't filled all the positions the new place can accommodate. We built this space to grow, and the Blackwood Bank account will allow us to do just that," Dane pointed out reasonably.

Kai blew out a frustrated breath, hating that his brother was right. Hating that he'd thought about Miranda almost nonstop since she'd walked out of his office the day before.

"Kai, you know that a partnership with Blackwood Bank would give Madtec that final stamp of legitimacy we've been looking for." Dane finally dropped into the seat across from Kai's desk. Dane sat forward in his chair. "CEOs from major corporations across the country would be willing to take a cue from an institution as prestigious as Blackwood to take a chance on a business founded by a couple of ex-hackers."

"The affiliation would take us mainstream," Kai admitted, knowing he couldn't deny Dane this opportunity to cast off the last taint of his jail time.

How ironic that Miranda had been the one to give them that chance.

"You'll sign?" Dane pressed.

Kai picked up the pen for an answer, seeing no

other choice. He'd bring the signed contracts to Miranda personally. Maybe then, he'd figure out a way to broker a peace between them long enough to fulfill Madtec's obligations to Blackwood Bank.

Dane was right about the need to accept the offer. But the sooner the job was done, the sooner Kai would put Miranda Dupree back in his past, where she belonged.

Miranda clutched a letter from Buckley Blackwood in her hands, eyes moving over the text. This was the third and final missive Buck had written to be delivered to her after his death. The first had explained the true intentions behind his will and the role he'd needed her to play. The second had included instructions on how to find his illegitimate son, Darius, and bring him into contact with the rest of the family. Now this letter included the last of his requests. She reread her ex-husband's final missive for her.

Dear Miranda,
Thank you for hanging in there with me to take care of these last tasks—the jobs I couldn't seem to pull off myself when I still had time. I hope this one last request will be a little easier than the others. I'd like you to organize a send-off for me, but not some schmaltzy memorial service—you know I hate things like that. I'm picturing an epic charity event, something

like "Royal Gives Back," and I want you to organize it as only you can. I was thinking the proceeds ought to go to the Stroke Foundation or maybe the Heart Association since they study the underlying causes of strokes. It still weighs on me that my children lost their mother too soon because of a stroke. I wasn't the husband I should have been to Donna-Leigh before our divorce, but I'd like to do this in her honor. Now that I've been exposed for a philanthropist do-gooder, I might as well go all out one last time, right? I know you won't disappoint me. After this last favor, you can go back to your life in New York, and I'll rest easier. Yours, Buck.

Miranda returned Buckley's last letter to the small secretary desk in the guesthouse's second bedroom that served as her temporary office. She mulled over what it meant as she sat in front her laptop to review her work email for Goddess. Kace LeBlanc had hand delivered the note this morning, assuring her it would be the final note from Buckley.

That had been both good and bad news for her. While she was relieved there would be no more surprises from her ex, she would also miss Royal. She'd grown close to her stepchildren, people who felt more like her family these days than her mother ever had. Her gaze shifted away from her laptop screen to a new framed photo of the Blackwood heirs from Sophie's wedding—Sophie, Kellan and Vaughn with their half brother, Darius. Buckley would be so proud to have them all together at last.

Miranda felt glad she'd played a part in making that happen. Buckley hadn't been a great father, but he'd cared. Miranda's father had died when she was three, too young to be sure she remembered him, although sometimes she imagined she recalled his laugh or a feeling of being hugged by him. At first, her mother had worked two jobs after his death to provide for them, but she'd given up by the time Miranda was ten. The house fell into disrepair. The electricity was shut off more often than not. Miranda had only ever worn other girls' cast-off clothes. None of which was as troubling as her mother's decision to spend the little bit of money she brought in on a prescription pill addiction.

Ginny Dupree was a mean addict. She didn't hit, but she threw things, and she was verbally cruel. Some of her more cutting words had continued to hurt Miranda long afterward, which was why she drew firm boundaries with her now. But as she saw the Blackwood family healing, Miranda couldn't help a twinge of envy for the kind of companionship and support that came with family relationships.

The love.

She suspected that lack of love in her childhood home had been one of the driving forces behind her strong feelings for Kai Maddox. Being with Kai had opened a whole new world of possibilities for her heart.

Until he'd started to withdraw from her. She'd never understood it, but she'd felt his retreat in the weeks before their split. He might blame her for their breakup, but he'd pulled away long before she'd ended things.

Buckley Blackwood might have been richer and worldlier than Kai. But in many ways, she'd settled for him when she'd married him, telling herself maybe her quieter, steadier feelings for him were what more mature love felt like.

Lesson learned.

Except Kai Maddox was back in her thoughts now, stirring up feelings she'd thought she'd put to rest long ago. And stirring up a hunger for him that she couldn't possibly deny. She'd dreamed about his hands all over her the night before, bringing her intense pleasure while he whispered wicked, suggestive things in her ear. She'd awoken edgy and breathless, her heart beating fast.

Maybe organizing this charity event for Buckley was just what she needed. Instead of spending her final month in Royal working side by side with an old lover she couldn't stop thinking about, she would spend it planning something worthwhile.

With a frustrated sigh, she shut her laptop and changed into her workout clothes, knowing she'd never get anything accomplished with her thoughts spinning this way.

* * *

Lying on her belly in cobra pose, Miranda arched her spine and pulled her shoulders back while she moved through her afternoon yoga workout in the studio of the Blackwood Hollow guesthouse. She inhaled deeply and slowly, matching her breath to her pose. The cycle of postures in the sun salutation was grounding for her during times of stress, and it took all her effort to focus on her breathing when memories of Kai clung to her thoughts.

With her mat positioned near the studio's big front window overlooking the grounds, she held the pose for five deep breaths, turning her head to one side and then the other as she tried not to think about how it had felt to stand near him. She would force his smoldering image from her mind by sheer will.

Except, was that him pulling into the driveway of the guesthouse? Parking a sleek silver sports car in front of the double bay detached garage?

She forgot all about her breath in the scramble to her feet as Kai emerged from a Jaguar F-Type coupe. Dressed in a deep blue jacket with a light blue shirt underneath, he looked more casual than the day before and every bit as compelling. Awareness and anticipation tingled over her skin. She had to remind herself that her sexy dream about him hadn't been real. That she couldn't afford to indulge those kinds of thoughts around him. She hurried toward the door, dismayed that instead of being dressed to impress, she wore capri-length leggings and a drapey tank shirt for her workout.

Not that there was any help for it now.

Slipping on a pair of beaded sandals by the front mat, Miranda opened the door of the studio attached to the rest of the guesthouse by a covered breezeway. The smooth stone path connected the buildings, outlined by native plants and shrubs. When she stepped outside, Kai's green gaze swung toward her.

He changed the trajectory of his stride, turning away from the main house toward the studio building. She hadn't realized until then he carried a small box with an all-too-recognizable logo on it.

One that stirred nostalgia.

"Hello, Miranda. I hope I didn't interrupt you." He stopped a few feet from her under the shade of the breezeway, the spring air still fragrant with almond verbena.

Her breath caught to be close to him again, her heart rate picking up speed.

"I'm surprised to see you." She remembered how curt he'd been the day before, but if he was here to tell her he'd reconsidered, she couldn't afford to refuse. Still, there was no reason to make it too easy for him. She'd had to scarf down humble pie the day before—it wouldn't kill him to have a bite or two of his own. "I got the distinct impression you didn't want to cross paths again when I left your office yesterday."

"For that, I apologize." He lifted the white box in his hands. "I brought a peace offering."

Her gaze shifted to the parcel with the Deer Springs Diner label, a million memories bombarding her all over again. She used to waitress there, depending on the money to finance her first yoga studio. She'd met Kai there. They'd spent time plotting to take over the world from their favorite booth in the corner, and had shared many breakfasts there after long nights of lovemaking. Tentatively, she lifted the lid.

She suspected what would be inside before she even peeked under the top.

"Half lemon meringue, half caramel apple," she confirmed, the scent of their two favorites stirring nostalgia and longing she couldn't afford to feel around this man. Part of her wanted to send him away, escape what he made her feel. But she still needed him on a professional level. "Would you like to come in for a slice?"

She peered up at him and realized how close they stood. Close enough for her to touch the short bristles he'd always worn along his jaw. Close enough to breathe in the light spice of soap on his olive-toned skin and remember the taste of him. Hastily, she released the box top and took a step back.

"Thank you. I'd like that very much." His green eyes missed nothing. "We can celebrate our new venture together since I have a signed contract to give you."

The surprises continued.

"That's excellent news." For the bank, of course. But for her, the prospect of working with him proved equal parts tempting and daunting. "Although I'll admit I'm curious what made you change your mind after you seemed so adamantly opposed yesterday. Was it the prospect of me stepping aside?"

Turning, she led the way to the front door of the guesthouse, aware of his nearness every step of the way.

"No. That won't be necessary. I can separate my personal life from my business obligations." He sounded sincere. And yet both times she'd visited him recently, there had been enough sensual tension simmering to burn them both. Did he plan to ignore it?

Giving herself a few heartbeats to shore up her boundaries, she entered the cool interior of the guesthouse and paused in the entryway as Kai pulled the door closed behind them. The dark wood floor and white walls were simply furnished with rustic elegance. Sturdy leather couches and heavy iron pendant lamps were softened by an abundance of natural light, pale rugs and oversize yellow throw pillows. Drinking in the calming effects, she glanced at him.

"I didn't expect a warm reception after how we parted ten years ago," she admitted, pulse skipping erratically as she continued toward the open kitchen to retrieve plates and forks. "And how you reacted to seeing me in New York."

She hoped discussing it would dismiss the elephant in the room. They needed to put their old relationship behind them, so it didn't interfere with the bank's business.

Kai joined her at the kitchen island, setting the pie box on the white quartz countertop.

"That's all in the past now. I was needlessly abrupt yesterday, especially when you came to discuss a significant opportunity for Madtec." He reached into an interior pocket of his jacket and retrieved a folded packet of papers. He laid them on the counter, as well. "Dane and I look forward to a thorough review and revamp of the bank's digital security."

Miranda retrieved two bottles of sparkling water from the refrigerator and placed them on a bamboo serving tray along with the plates and silverware. While it would be easy to eat indoors at the kitchen counter, she thought sitting under the pergola in the backyard would help her keep boundaries in place. Especially when lemon meringue and caramel apple pie slices had the power to catapult her back in time to that diner with Kai. Feeding each other bites. Sitting so close her thigh pressed against his.

She would *not* think about his thighs.

"Dane convinced you to give this a chance?" she guessed aloud, her cheeks warm from the vivid thoughts she was trying to stifle.

"He was livid I hadn't already signed the papers," Kai acknowledged. As she moved to pick up the tray, he took over the task, his warm hand brushing hers momentarily. "Lead the way."

She felt that brief touch long afterward. *Breathe in. Breathe out.* She opened the French doors to the patio where coral honeysuckle hung from the deep pergola. Hummingbirds bobbed around the vibrant trumpet-shaped blooms. Kai set the tray on the wrought iron dining table, then pulled out a cushioned chair for Miranda.

"Thank you." She tried to recall the thread of the conversation to distract herself from all the ways his nearness affected her. "I hope that Dane's insistence doesn't mean you're conflicted about working with us."

"I have no trouble opposing my brother when the situation calls for it." Kai took the seat next to her at the round table. "But in this case, Dane's instincts were correct. The software we're developing is tailor-made for a complex financial platform like Blackwood Bank."

Grounding herself in mundane tasks, Miranda laid out napkins and divvied up the waters while Kai opened the pie box and slid thin slices onto their plates. One of each kind for each of them. But rather than soothing her with routine, the familiarity of that simple act, something they'd done countless times and yet not for so many years, crowded her chest with feelings she wasn't ready for. Swallowing past the swell of emotion, she took her time smoothing the napkin over her lap.

"I have followed the rise of Madtec with interest. I suspected your company was a good fit for this role, Kai, or I wouldn't have approached you." She appreciated how the conversation anchored her in the purpose of the meeting. Because this was just business.

Something they both excelled at. Unlike personal relationships.

"I know that," he conceded, lifting his water bottle and clinking it lightly to hers. "Thank you."

Her gaze flicked to his as he held the pale green bottle in midair. She followed suit, clinking hers to his in a friendly toast that felt like a fresh start.

At least, professionally speaking.

"Here's to a successful partnership." Kai's green gaze lingered on hers, and she couldn't help but think she saw something simmering in their depths.

Old frustration over how things had ended? Or a hint of the lingering attraction that she'd been grappling with all day?

Neither one boded well for their venture. But she licked her lips before raising the bottle to her mouth. One way or another, she would figure out how to work with Kai Maddox for the sake of Blackwood Bank. "To new beginnings."

Three

She had the sexiest mouth he'd ever seen on a woman.

Kai tried not to stare at it, the top lip slightly fuller than the bottom in a perfect cupid's bow that made her look perpetually ready for a kiss. But the more he tried not to think about that incredible mouth of hers, the more he pictured it doing wicked things to him.

Being seated across from Miranda on a property that had once belonged to his rival for her affections felt damned surreal.

Kai had made the trip into Royal with his best professional intentions, hoping to make peace enough to take care of business together. But one look at her in the afternoon sunlight with no makeup on, wearing her yoga clothes, had stolen the breath from his lungs. Miranda was a beautiful woman no matter what. Full stop. Yet seeing her relaxed in her temporary home had reminded him of the woman he'd known, before she was a business mogul in her own right. The sight had catapulted him a decade backward in time, right down to wishing he could invite her for a ride on the back of his motorcycle, her slender thighs hugging his hips.

Except they were far different people now, no matter if he still saw shades of the woman he'd once loved in Miranda. That woman had been a myth—an illusion fueled by incredible chemistry. She'd made that clear when she left him for Buckley.

"We should discuss our next steps," he suggested as he pushed aside his plate. "The contract put a very condensed timeline in place for updating the bank's cybersecurity."

He glanced around to ensure their privacy. The patio behind the Blackwood Hollow guesthouse had a large, covered area for entertaining, complete with fireplace and outdoor kitchen. The table under the vine-covered pergola looked out over the pool shared with the main house. There was no one in sight.

Miranda nodded, bringing his attention back to the moment. To her. A few tendrils of red hair slipped from the clip holding the rest at her nape. "Because I have a reason to worry about it. Most aspects of the bank have been well managed since Buckley's death, but the internal data security director has flagged several concerns that haven't been addressed."

"The outside company Blackwood contracted with prior to us has had a few incidents in the past two years, which suggests to me they are failing to stay up-to-date." Kai had spot-checked Blackwood's system before making the trip to Royal to start familiarizing himself. "Our service niche requires continual, aggressive measures to keep current in a quickly changing marketplace."

"You and Dane have done incredibly well for yourselves, especially—" Her tone suggested she'd been about to say more but she stopped abruptly, then glanced back down at her plate. She speared her fork through a morsel of lemon meringue pie.

"Especially for former hackers?" he supplied, knowing he'd guessed accurately by the slightest tinge of pink in her cheeks. "You can't be a success at preventing cybercrime without knowing how the criminal element works."

"Madtec's rapid rise has been formidable," she amended before sliding her dessert dish to one side. "But remembering how protective you were of Dane, I know that it had to be hard for you when he got into legal trouble."

His jaw tightened. While he felt a small amount of satisfaction that she'd noticed Dane's arrest even as she'd been celebrating her engagement, Kai couldn't dodge the sting of resentment, too. He'd been solely responsible for his brother since their father died of pancreatic cancer when Kai was seventeen and Dane was fifteen. Their mom had been exhausted from the hardship of caregiving and her own grief, and she'd taken off to recover, leaving Kai in charge. She never returned.

"Mostly, I regretted that I hadn't been giving him my full attention in the months before his arrest. He'd only just turned eighteen." Instead of working with his brother on the weekend of the hacking incident that had first flagged an investigation into his brother's activities, he'd taken Miranda to Galveston for a few days at the beach even though her mother had already told Kai that Buckley Blackwood had started coming around the Dupree house. Kai had thought maybe devoting more attention to her would sway things in his favor, but in the end, he couldn't compete with Buckley's money.

Did she remember the timing of the events leading to Dane's arrest? It had been some months after the investigation began, but surely she remembered he'd been concerned about his brother's activities when Kai hadn't been around to keep an eye on him.

Her blue gaze broke away from his. Retrieving her water bottle, she took a long drink. "Dane was a prodigy. When someone is so gifted intellectually, it's probably easy to lose sight of their youth."

Leaning back in his chair, he weighed her answer. Told himself not to ruminate on the past. And still found himself asking, "Speaking of family, how's your mother?"

Her lips pressed together momentarily. A fleeting reaction from this self-contained woman, but he didn't miss it. He'd never understood the dynamic between her and her mom, but then again, Miranda had been more focused on her future than her past when they'd dated.

"Honestly, I'm not sure." She folded the linen napkin that had been on her lap, matching the corners and smoothing the fabric. "She has battled an addiction to prescription painkillers over the years, and that's made it difficult for us to maintain a relationship."

"I'm so sorry to hear it." The news was unexpected. Jarring, even, considering Ginny Dupree had been the one to warn Kai away from her daughter. Had she been an untrustworthy source of information? "I never saw any sign of that kind of problem when we were dating."

"She used to hide it better than she does now," Miranda told him drily, moving the folded napkin to the table and laying it over her plate. "But the problem dates back to when I was a preteen. I started working at a young age since a lot of her paycheck went toward her problems."

His understanding of their past together shifted, the pieces falling together in a different way. Had Miranda's financial situation pushed her toward Buckley? Or had her mother seen a payday when the wealthy rancher had come calling?

It didn't matter now since their breakup had been so long ago. But damn.

"I always admired your ambition, but I didn't realize that it was partially driven by necessity." He reached across the table to lay his hand on hers before considering the wisdom of it, the movement instinctive.

Her blue eyes darted to his, awareness leaping between them when he'd meant only to offer empathy. Understanding.

"Circumstances help make us who we are—good or bad." She didn't move her hand beneath his fingers, but he could feel the leap of her pulse at the base of her thumb. Her skin was so soft. "I'd like to think I used her problems as a push in a positive direction for myself."

He forced himself to release her, but it took more effort than it should have. And he may have glided a touch along the pulse point of her wrist before letting go completely, wanting her to remember the way they could set each other on fire.

Her eyes darted to his. Aware. He didn't know what to make of the current sparking between them. No matter how much he wanted to tell himself this next phase of their relationship needed to be all business, he was still undeniably drawn to her. He wanted to know more about her and how she'd spent the last ten years, but since he suspected she wasn't any more eager to talk about her past than he was willing to revisit his, he let go of the topic.

"That sounds like some of the inspiration for your nonprofit." While Kai hadn't watched much of her reality television show, he had pulled up a speech she'd given about her charity when he'd seen a mention of it online a year ago. "I read about Girl to the Nth Power."

She'd organized the group five years ago and had since received national service awards for her efforts to create supportive environments for young women. In her speech, she'd referred to her organization as a girls' club for a new generation, complete with mentors in disciplines from the arts to STEM, with access to workshops on friendship and self-care.

Her whole face changed, her expression lighting with some of that ambition and passion he remembered from those conversations in the diner where they'd shared their dreams. "While I'm incredibly proud of the work I do at Goddess, Girl to the Nth Power is where my heart lies. It's exciting to make a difference in teens' lives."

He couldn't miss the spark in her eyes. The commitment to her cause.

"If your schedule permits, you should come down to the community center in Deer Springs sometime. Check out the afterschool program." He thought she might be interested in the operation because of her work with teens. Not because he wanted her to spend more time near him.

"I read something about the community center." She stacked their dishes back on the tray they'd used to carry everything outside.

Taking his cue from her, he lifted the tray and followed her back inside the house, his gaze dropping to her curves as she moved. A butterfly tattoo on the back of one ankle was a colorful new addition that called him to explore the rest of her. He placed the tray on the island and shoved his hands in his pockets to remind them not to wander.

"Dane and I built one at the same time we broke ground on the Madtec headquarters. We thought it would give back to the town and make it more inviting for potential employees." He liked the idea of giving local teens more support and opportunities than he and Dane had.

"Smart thinking of you." She slid the remnants of the pie in the refrigerator while he loaded the plates in the dishwasher. "And thank you for the invitation. I'd like to see the community center."

Sensing their time together was coming to an end, Kai wouldn't linger. It was enough to give her the signed contract and pave the way for a working relationship. No need to rehash the past.

"Excellent. We'll be in touch with the Blackwood Bank data security director today and get to work installing new encryption precautions." He should shake her hand and leave. Or maybe just leave.

Except spending time with her today had stirred up too much. His feet didn't move as he watched her lean a hip against the kitchen island.

"I'm glad you changed your mind about handling the cybersecurity, Kai," she admitted. "Thank you."

Walk away, his brain told him.

But he didn't think he could keep this facade of

civility between them every time they saw one another if he didn't address at least one of the issues
that still bugged the hell out of him after all this time.

"Kai?" Her brow furrowed as she looked up at
him questioningly.

Standing there together in that quiet kitchen could
have been any one of a hundred times they'd been
alone. The past and the present merged.

"There's just one more thing." He shifted closer,
lowering his voice. "It's strange for me to be in
Blackwood Hollow with you after how things ended
for us. But how does it feel for you to be living in
Buckley's guesthouse and overseeing his estate surrounded by his sons and daughter?"

She bristled visibly. "I'm not their enemy. Buckley
arranged for me to play a role helping them through
the aftermath of his death."

"Still loyal to him even after the divorce?" The
question came out crueler than he'd intended. But he
couldn't help wanting to know.

Her eyes narrowed and she straightened from the
island.

"That's not any of your business," she told him
coolly, making it clear that he'd effectively erased
any progress he'd made smoothing things over between them.

"You're right, it isn't," he agreed, suspecting he'd
need Dane to be the one to interact with Blackwood
Bank if Kai couldn't refrain from poking at the past
this way. "But that doesn't take away the fact that

things are bound to be awkward between us while we're finding our footing to make this deal work."

Her full lips pursed. She gave a clipped nod and leaned toward him.

"In that case, let me assure you that living here again is beyond strange for me." She stabbed one manicured finger into the quartz countertop to make her point, a diamond tennis bracelet quivering with the movement. "Discovering my ex-husband trusted me with all his worldly assets during this transition of power to his kids has been even more bizarre." Another finger stabbing the quartz. "But given how much time has passed since you and I shared a history, I don't think there's any need for *awkwardness.* I'm thirty-six years old, Kai. I don't do awkward."

He welcomed the passionate outpouring from her, another facet of Miranda he recognized better than the self-possessed control she'd exhibited in his office and throughout some of their talk today. He stifled the urge to smile at the reemergence of her fiery side.

"Point taken. I've long envied your maturity," he told her with 100 percent honesty. "But for what it's worth, I think what I'm labeling 'awkwardness' might be more accurately called *attraction.*" He gave her a moment to process that, knowing he owed her the truth even if it made a working relationship more difficult to navigate. "I'll be on my best behavior with you, Miranda, but I think it's obvious the fire is still there."

This time, she had no comeback, her lips parted in surprise.

Hell, he'd shocked himself too with that admission. But he wasn't the kind of guy to sidestep the facts. He plowed straight through.

Now, he watched as her jaw snapped shut and she straightened.

"Then maybe we should wait for things to cool off and revisit this at a later date." She stalked past him toward the front door, clearly done with him for the day. She pulled it open and stood to one side of the exit, studying him. "Goodbye, Kai."

Had he overstepped the bounds of professionalism?

He didn't think so. She knew him well, no matter that their shared history was ten years old. She couldn't be too surprised that he would speak plainly about his feelings. The attraction was still there—it would be ridiculous to pretend otherwise.

Closing the distance between them, he moved toward the door. He stopped before stepping over the threshold, their gazes meeting.

"Come to Deer Springs," he urged, awareness of her inching over his skin. "If we can come to terms with the history between us, then we can get some closure. Maybe then the attraction will fade and it will be easier to work together."

Her breathing quickened, the stroke of each warm puff stirring an answering heat inside him. But he didn't wait for her to agree. He strode by her toward his vehicle, needing to put Miranda in his rearview mirror. Not just today.

This time, for good.

Three days later, Miranda sat outside on the guest-house patio with her morning coffee and set aside her work to organize the Royal Gives Back gala that Buckley wanted. Instead, she scrolled through the latest photos from Sophie Blackwood Townshend's European honeymoon. Sophie, the baby of the Black-wood family, had married Miranda's producer last month and was living it up in Paris, Morocco and—most recently—Florence. The backdrop in every pic-ture was stunning, but what captured Miranda's eye most was how in love the happy couple looked. So-phie had met Nigel while working under a false iden-tity at Green Room Media in New York in an effort to dig up dirt on Miranda. Happily, she'd found noth-ing and had finally come to terms with their relation-ship. It touched Miranda's heart to be included on the family's message group each day and see what Sophie was up to.

Although, settling her phone back on the wrought iron table, Miranda had to admit that even as her comfort with the Blackwoods grew, the contrast made her more aware of how she'd failed to heal the rift with her mother.

Maybe she didn't need to since her mom had betrayed the most basic rules of family loyalty in the past. But since Ginny Dupree was an addict,

Miranda still held out hope one day it might be different between them.

Kai's suggestion she visit Deer Springs echoed in her mind—along with his reminder about the attraction that still simmered. At first, she'd been angry with him for stirring up trouble. Yet a part of her couldn't help but admire his willingness to wade headlong into the topics most people would dance around. It made things frustrating since it would be more comfortable to pretend the spark they'd shared was long buried. But was it true?

She couldn't deny the flare of heat when he'd touched her, even in a moment intended to offer comfort. Maybe he had a good point about trying to get closure. Surely then she could put all her feelings for him behind her. But every time she thought about him saying it was obvious the fire between them was still there, her belly flipped just like it had the first time they'd met.

Miranda had been holding down two jobs at the time, overloaded by the lunch crowd in the diner where she worked as a waitress, and panicked about the duct tape holding together a split seam in her uniform, a tear she hadn't gotten around to sewing the day before after getting into an argument with her mother. She'd never forget how it felt to arrive at Kai's table to take his order and having his heart-stopping smile chase away all the stress until it evaporated like summer dew.

He'd insisted he didn't want to order until she

could join him for lunch. She'd brought him a soda anyway. He hadn't touched it until two o'clock when her shift ended. After she took a seat, it seemed like they didn't stop talking for months except to kiss and make love.

But Kai ended things.

Not in so many words, of course. But in his actions. He'd been the one to retreat.

She'd always thought it was stress of his own that had made him pull away. He'd worked even more hours than she had, and some of the jobs had been shady. And yes, that had bothered her, given how many times she'd been burned by her mother's brand of flexible ethics. She'd had enough instability in her life. She wanted steady. Even if predictable wasn't some people's idea of happily ever after, to her it had sounded blissful. Kai was six years younger than her, and he lived more dangerously than Miranda ever could. And yet she'd put up with all of that, compromising again and again, until she'd felt him pulling away. That was when she'd decided to stop trying.

He hadn't even argued with her when she'd decided to end things, the final proof she'd needed that things weren't right between them. Was it any wonder she'd been aggravated two days ago by his insinuations of loyalty to Buckley?

The marriage hadn't been perfect, but she'd given it her best shot.

Leaving her coffee cup on the patio table, Miranda grabbed her phone and put it in her pocket.

She wasn't going to get anything accomplished on the Royal Gives Back event with her thoughts straying time and again to Kai.

He'd invited her to Deer Springs to put the past behind them, hadn't he? She intended to take him up on it.

Four

Lulu Shepard raised her fist to knock on the door of the guesthouse when Miranda opened it wide.

"Lulu." Miranda smiled warmly, wrapping her in a friendly hug that carried a whiff of subtle perfume. "I wasn't expecting you. Is everything okay?"

Stressed and anxious about her wedding plans, Lulu hoped Miranda could help her. Sometimes she wondered if the other woman had ever experienced a moment's indecision. She seemed so perpetually poised.

Designer purse in hand, Miranda wore a fitted navy blue suit with wide lapels. Raspberry-colored sling back heels were a nice touch. Miranda always managed to look feminine and badass at the same time.

"I'm fine. I just wanted some wedding advice, but

I won't keep you if you're on your way out." Lulu stepped back, giving her friend room to join her on the porch.

Pulling the door closed behind her, Miranda pointed to a couple of Adirondack chairs to one side. "I always have time for you. Let's sit."

Relieved, Lulu dropped into one of the seats. "Thank you. I'm in a dilemma about the bridesmaids for my wedding. I worked out the details with your stepson and then Nigel texted me confirmation that we can have the wedding here at Blackwood Hollow, which is great. But he sent around a memorandum to the crew that our next episode will be shopping for bridesmaid dresses for all of the *Secret Lives* members."

"I remember seeing that," Miranda confirmed. "And I'm glad you're getting married here, but I do remember thinking that it's going to seem forced for you to have us in your wedding. The audience knows we're not all best friends."

Lulu bit her lip, hoping she hadn't offended Miranda, whom she'd grown close to over the last two seasons. "I want Fee, of course, and I'd love to have you in it, but Rafaela? Come on. Why would I ask her to stand up with me after some of the stunts she's pulled?"

Earlier in the season, Rafaela Marchesi had snapped a photo of Seraphina's fiancé, rancher Clint Rockwell, without his prosthetic leg and sent it to the media in an obvious bid for ratings. Fee had been hurt and furious, of course, so as Fee's best friend, Lulu had been doubly outraged. She still was. She'd go to the mat for Fee.

"You have every right to decide who you want in your wedding," Miranda assured her in no uncertain terms, stabbing the arm of the chair with an emphatic finger. "That's a given. But it occurs to me that maybe Nigel is setting us up for the usual show drama by putting you in the position of having to tell the others yourself—on camera."

"Meaning you think he wants a bridesmaid shopping show to turn into a bitch-fest about exactly that kind of thing?" Lulu hadn't considered that, but it made perfect sense.

"If I've learned one thing from doing this series, it's that we live or die by the sound bites." Miranda shrugged a shoulder. "That's why I don't get as much screen time. I'm less interesting for viewers because I don't go from zero to sixty with my emotions."

"Or with your mouth," Lulu added, thinking how grounded Miranda seemed. How unlikely to fly off the handle. Whereas the others—Lulu included— were all apt to say whatever came to mind. They didn't hold back.

"Exactly," Miranda agreed, leaning back in her seat with a thoughtful expression. "Still waters might run deep, but they don't make for good television. I'm okay with that, though. I'm grateful to be a part of the show for the friendships. I hadn't realized until

I got involved with *Secret Lives* how lacking my life has been in female friendships."

Touched, Lulu squeezed Miranda's hand. "I'm glad to have you in my life, too," she told her honestly, appreciating the different perspective. "What would you do about the bridesmaids if you were me?"

"The simplest option would be to just go along with it. You wouldn't be the first woman to fill up her wedding photos with frenemies. At least with us, you'll be aware of what to expect. How many friends do you know who were coerced to put cousins they hardly knew in their ceremony in order to placate an aunt or mother—only to then get in trouble anyway when the cousin couldn't stand the other bridesmaids? We've gotten through a few seasons and haven't killed each other yet, so you'll be safe on that score." Miranda shrugged, making it all sound so reasonable. "Personally, I don't think it's a big deal to have Rafaela in your wedding photos, but it's not about me, Lu. It's your day. Yours and Kace's."

Lulu's heart warmed all over again at the thought of marrying Kace. Having the day free of drama and artifice had become so very important. This was about their future. Their love. Not ratings.

"And at the end of the day, that's all that really matters, isn't it?" Lulu felt a tension slide away at Miranda's gentle wisdom and she decided she needed some more of that brand of Zen in her life. Or maybe she was already experiencing it now that she felt loved and appreciated by a man she wanted to spend the rest of her life with. "At my first wedding, I got all spun up about the details—seating arrangements and a whole lot of superficial stuff that didn't really matter."

"What counts is the marriage, not the wedding." Lulu caught the shadows in her friend's eyes. Was she thinking of her own marriage to Buckley?

Lulu knew Miranda hadn't had an easy road, no matter how much of a placid facade she tried to present to the world.

"I'm going to do it right this time," Lulu agreed, already imagining the future she'd have waking beside Kace every day. "The marriage, that is."

Miranda nodded approvingly, a few darting birds chirping a happy echo to the sentiment. "I know it's right when I see you two together. I think it's obvious to everyone around you."

Lulu held tight to the knowledge. She didn't need anyone else's approval, but she liked the idea that her friends backed her decision. "He makes me happy." It was as simple as that. "And the wedding can be as over-the-top as Nigel wants it."

"Are you sure?" Miranda asked, leaning forward, a diamond pendant swinging out and reflecting the sun. "Because you can tell him that you don't want Rafaela—or any of us—in it."

"I'm sure." At peace with her decision, she accepted that the wedding was a one-day party. The marriage was what would last a lifetime. "I wouldn't have met Kace without this show, and I don't mind celebrating that. Once the reception is over, I'm going to have a good man in my life forever, and that's what counts."

Standing, she thanked Miranda for helping her think things through. Before she left, however, she couldn't help but ask, "Where are you headed? That suit looks stunning on you."

Even before Miranda answered, Lulu's instincts told her Miranda was going to see a man. There was a hesitation. The briefest moment of uncertainty that Lulu didn't remember ever seeing before in this supremely poised woman.

"I'm heading to Deer Springs to speak with the tech company helping me bring Blackwood Bank's security up to speed." Miranda rose, walking Lulu to her rental car.

"My female intuition is screaming that there's a person of interest on the other end of this meeting," Lulu said lightly, not expecting much of a reply. Trying to pin Miranda down wouldn't yield results anyway.

Opening the driver's side door, Lulu remembered clearly how it felt to be circling Kace when they were getting to know one another. How alive she felt. She still did, just thinking about him.

She hoped Miranda's mystery man was worthy of her.

"He's interesting, all right," Miranda admitted, standing by the tall pots of flowering trees that lined the porch. "I'll give him that."

Lulu whistled low under her breath as she started the car, intrigued at the thought of Miranda navigating a new relationship. "For what it's worth, you look sizzling hot. Thank you for the advice, Miranda."

"Always," Miranda assured her, closing the driver's door before blowing her a kiss as Lulu put the car in Reverse.

Her heart felt happy. She would have Seraphina as her maid of honor in her wedding. As for Rafaela, Lulu knew Miranda would be right there next to her to intervene if their fame-chasing costar stepped out of line. Because while the audience might see Miranda as the grounded one who didn't cause a stir, Lulu had no doubt that her quieter friend would do whatever was necessary to make sure the wedding went smoothly. She just hoped Miranda knew that her friends would have her back in return, no matter what she was going through on her own.

Kai had just finished helping one of the kids in his coding class at the community center when a teen in the back of the room let out a quiet wolf whistle.

"Is there a problem, Rhys?" he asked the boy seated closest to the window. The teen's eyes were fixed on something outside in the parking lot.

Normally, Kai had the blinds lowered since the first-floor tech room had a view of people coming and going from the building, but today he'd opened one to let in some natural light.

"Sorry," Rhys muttered, swiveling in his chair to face his laptop screen. "Got distracted."

The teen went back to work without Kai having to say anything else, and Kai was about to dismiss the class when he spotted a feminine figure striding closer to the building's front doors.

Miranda.

Anticipation fired through him, even as he experienced a moment of understanding for the teen student's loss of focus. No doubt, Miranda had the power to distract. She entered the community center's front doors, out of sight once more.

"We'll finish our projects next time," Kai announced. "The tech lab will remain open for another hour if anyone wants to keep working."

Kai nodded his thanks to the lab's afternoon monitor, a local graduate student earning some internship credits. About half of the students gathered their backpacks and dispersed to the gym or the game lounge, but the rest stayed behind, including the wolf whistler.

Kai clapped Rhys on the shoulder before leaving the class. "Whistles and catcalling can make women uncomfortable," he reminded. The kid was working on a sophisticated program for someone his age—but when it came to emotional maturity, he still had a lot to learn. "A definite no-go."

"It won't happen again," Rhys assured him quickly, straightening in his chair.

Nodding, Kai let the kid off the hook, then headed

toward the door to find Miranda. He could only assume she was here because she'd taken him up on the offer to put the past behind them in the town where they'd met. The town where their affair had set them both on fire.

He spotted her just outside the tech lab door, her fitted blue suit skimming her memorable curves, the skirt revealing toned legs. Hunger for her stirred. Not just because she was an extremely attractive woman. Some of his best memories were with her at his side.

"Hello, Kai." She tucked a slim handbag under one arm, her gaze fixed on his.

"I wasn't sure you'd come." He'd been waiting for days, wondering if he'd overstepped by suggesting they had unfinished business between them.

"I wasn't either," she admitted, her gaze taking in the huge common area of the community center. Couches were filled with groups of teens talking and laughing. The area was ringed by meeting rooms, a game room, gym and a snack counter. "When it comes to a business decision, I'm sure of myself. But the way forward in my personal life never seems quite as clear."

He appreciated her honesty, and repaid her in kind. "I'm glad you're here."

While it might be easier for them both, from a business perspective, to ignore their history for the sake of Blackwood Bank, Kai found himself wanting more resolution with Miranda. Or did he just want to bring her home with him and forget all the animosity to lose himself in her one last time? He couldn't deny that his thoughts about her ranged from sensual to explicit, and those thoughts were more and more frequent.

"You've done an amazing job with this place," she observed, not paying attention to the small commotion she was creating with her presence. A few girls seemed to have recognized Miranda's famous face, and the news spread in audible whispered conversations from group to group.

"Thank you. But it seems I've underestimated your show's popularity with the teen crowd. Looks like I created quite a stir by inviting you here." He slid a hand under her elbow, guiding her away from the lounge toward an unused meeting space in the back of the building. "Would you consider continuing our discussion at my house? I live close by."

She glanced over her shoulder briefly, as if to gauge how much of a commotion she was causing. Yet she never slowed her step, allowing him to lead her away.

A surge of misplaced possessiveness—or perhaps it was simple desire—made him want to wrap her in his arms. Tuck her even closer.

"Perhaps that would be for the best," she agreed, her voice quiet beside him so that he had to lean nearer to hear. "I'm parked out front."

"I'll drive you," he assured her, as he quickened his pace through the empty room sometimes used for local speakers or book clubs. There was a back entrance that opened onto a separate parking area. "My vehicle is right outside."

Today, no one else was in the rear lot as there were no special events planned for the evening, so they arrived at his Jaguar quickly enough.

"This is the second time I've seen you without a motorcycle," Miranda observed lightly while he unlocked the passenger door and opened it for her. "I will confess I'm surprised to see you behind the wheel of a car."

Watching her lower herself gracefully into the leather seat, Kai latched onto the topic of discussion to distract himself from her legs.

"While the Bluetooth systems available in helmets have come a long way, it's still easier to conduct a business call from a car," he admitted, closing her door and then letting himself into the driver's side. He started the engine once they were buckled in, heading west toward his house through the relatively quiet streets. "However, if you have an urge to roam Deer Springs on the back of a bike, it would be a pleasure to take you for a ride. I still keep two of them in the garage for when the restless urge strikes."

He shifted into a higher gear, remembering the feel of her arms wrapped around him, her breasts pressed against his back when they used to ride together. As her throaty laugh floated between them, he wondered if she was recalling some of those same times.

"I thought we were going to put the past to rest,

not relive it." She slanted a glance his way, blue eyes assessing.

That's what he'd thought, too.

But his relationship with Miranda had never lacked for complications. And he found himself tossing out a far thornier solution.

"There's more than one way to fix a simmering awareness." He knew better than to label the chemistry "awkwardness" this time. She'd been very clear about that. "We could appease it."

Just saying the words made the idea shimmer with real possibility. If she agreed, they could indulge themselves as much as they wanted. Let the heat consume them both. Visions of her naked and eager for him practically crowded out his view of the road.

"I don't think I can appease your restless urges, Kai." She shifted in her seat, crossing one leg over the other in a way that snagged his gaze. "I never was very effective at that. And now that we're older…"

She let the thought slide, as if he knew the rest of what she'd say. He had to refocus on the words since his brain lingered on her legs. He wanted to part her thighs and lay between them. Kiss her until they were both breathless.

"Now that we're older, what?" he prompted, needing her to spell it out for him while he battled enticing images in his head. He turned down a side street that led to his private drive.

"If I couldn't keep your attention when I was a twenty-six-year-old, chances are good I won't be enough of a diversion for you at thirty-six." Her words were so unexpected—so unwelcome and wrong—that he pulled to a stop the moment he turned onto his private driveway even though they hadn't reached the house yet.

He shoved the car in Park.

"You were all I could think about when you were twenty-six, Miranda." Hell, thinking about her to the exclusion of all else was what had cost Dane his freedom. That had been the final blow to their faltering relationship. "Holding my attention has never a problem for you."

Surprise colored her eyes, her expression thoughtful for a moment before she spoke.

"You checked out on our relationship long before I ended things," she reminded him.

"Only because I knew we were a lost cause once your mother told me Buckley Blackwood had started coming around." He'd never forget the force of that blow. The kindness shaded with pity in Ginny Dupree's eyes when she'd informed him he had a powerful—rich—rival for Miranda's affections. "Six weeks later, we were finished. Dane was under investigation. Buckley Blackwood was shopping for diamonds and you were out of my life for good."

He heard Miranda's quick gasp. Saw her brow furrow. But she knew how that story turned out as well as he did, so he couldn't imagine what she seemed surprised about now.

For his part, he welcomed the reminder that this meeting between them wasn't about appeasing the damnable attraction that hadn't faded. Better to confront it. Shred it apart if necessary.

One way or another, he was putting Madtec and his brother first this time. He wouldn't let his attraction get in the way. If it was a problem for her, then Miranda would have to figure out how to work with him. She'd always been good at prioritizing the bottom line ahead of everything else.

Miranda had come to Deer Springs to put the past to rest.

The idea had sounded a whole lot more peaceful than the process was turning out to be.

She'd made a misstep marrying Buckley—she could admit that now. Had it been rooted in her relationship with Kai? She'd forgotten how being with Kai had always felt like someone turned the flame on high beneath her normally mild emotions. With him, feelings were more intense. Anger and passion were hotter. Pleasure deeper. Hurts more painful. She'd have to sequester herself in her yoga studio to breathe through all the tumultuous sensations pinballing around inside her.

But the revelation that her mother had intervened with Kai—effectively chasing him off the moment Buckley had shown up at the Dupree house to ask if he could see Miranda privately—had rocked her. Kai had never told her about that before, but it made so many other perplexing moments from the past suddenly make sense.

Not that it mattered now.

As Kai drove the Jaguar the rest of the way down a winding drive and through a wrought iron gate flanked by brick columns, Miranda reminded herself to focus on the present. She needed to smooth things over with the copresident of Madtec and pave the way for a good working relationship with Blackwood Bank. That was why she was here.

Not to contemplate motorcycle rides with a hot guy from her past. Not even when he'd told her that she had been all he could think about back when they'd dated.

Pull it together.

"Here we are," he announced pulling around a copse of trees so she could see a house.

An incredible, modern marvel of a house. Because as the car arrived in the driveway, the lights around the place—inside and out—turned on.

"It's beautiful, Kai," she told him honestly, taking in the expanses of glass between sleek black stone walls.

The lights—perhaps motion-detection or connected to whatever security system he had in place—made the whole place glow. She could see into the huge rooms decorated in minimalist style. Designed in an L shape, the house wrapped around a pool that became visible only as he drove deeper into the property toward a detached garage. He didn't open any of the bays, however, leaving the sports coupe parked outside while she took in the details of the house.

A second-floor deck with a firepit and hot tub overlooked the pool area. From master suite to kitchen, guest rooms to office, the whole floor plan was visible thanks to the windows and abundant light.

"Thank you." He shut off the engine and came around to help her out of the car. "I worked on the design for almost a year before I was happy with it."

She braced herself for his touch before placing her hand in his, that current of awareness ever-present. Rising to her feet, she withdrew her hand quickly, but the memory of how he felt lingered long after.

Her only consolation was that Kai seemed ready to drop the idea of acting on their attraction after their conversation in the car.

"You designed this?" She shouldn't be surprised. She'd always known he was a gifted Renaissance man, his agile mind hopping from one project to the next, fascinated by the inner workings of things and studying them until he found answers that satisfied him.

"It was easier that way." His hand landed at the base of her spine briefly, guiding her toward a walkway leading around the pool. "At first, whenever I wanted to modify someone else's design to use recycled materials, I got a long song and dance about why it wouldn't work."

The feel of his touch called to her. She refocused

on the house, grounding herself in the physical space to keep her thoughts off the ever-present awareness of the man.

"So you developed your own design instead." She admired the black, glittering stone walls, idly wondering where he'd sourced the material.

Small talk was a whole lot easier than what she'd come here to discuss.

"It's my home. Why should I compromise?" A hint of a smile curved one side of his lips. "Although my builder did call my blueprints the most obnoxiously detailed he'd ever seen, I took it as a compliment that the end product is exactly what I'd envisioned."

He stopped in front of a sliding door that opened into the kitchen, and de-armed the security system with an app on his phone. The system chimed twice before he slid the door wide, then wider still, opening the wall to the outdoor area and letting in a warm breeze. The lights that had flickered to life while they were still in the driveway dimmed now, leaving only the pendant lamps in the kitchen, which Kai had flicked on with a conventional switch.

"You did an incredible job. Your house, Madtec, the community center—they're all a testament to how much you've invested in Deer Springs. The town must be very happy with you." She set her purse on a padded barstool with sleek chrome legs that was tucked under the marble island.

Kai retrieved a pair of small bottles of seltzer from

the built-in refrigerator and set them on the island near two glasses.

"This community was good to Dane and me after our father died and our mother left." He'd never spoken much about his family when they'd dated, but Miranda knew that his mom had taken off not long after their father had lost his protracted battle with cancer. "I had a lot of anger about my dad's passing and the responsibilities that came with my mom's departure, but the people here gave me room to work through it, overlooking a few screwups, helping out when they could."

"You've paid them back and then some," she assured him. "You've done good work here."

He dismissed her words with a curt shake of his head as he poured their drinks and passed her a glass while she thought back to their first meeting. It had been only three years after losing his parents, but he'd been so sharp. Mature beyond his age. Ready to take on the world.

She hated to think her mother had helped sabotage things between them when Kai already had so much on his plate. He'd had big dreams to build his company and advance his software. Except he'd had to look out for his younger brother.

Of course, Kai could have opted to fight for their relationship, and he hadn't. Sipping the bubbling water, Miranda's eyes met his over the rim of her glass. The bubbly sensation shifted from her lips to her belly, the awareness of him tickling over her skin.

It made no sense that he could make her feel like that from nothing more than a shared look. No doubt it had to do with the way he affected her, turning up the intensity of everything she felt. She set her glass aside abruptly, trying to rein in her emotions.

"Speaking of good work." He rested his glass on the counter beside hers and covered her fingers with his. "How do you suggest we move forward, Miranda, when the thought of kissing you crowds out everything else?"

Five

Miranda stilled.

He felt that stillness where he touched her, an unmoving wariness that lasted a long, breathless moment before her pulse jumped hard enough for him to feel the kick of it under his thumb.

"You were never one to mince words," she said finally, her blue gaze tracking his, probing deeper as if she could pluck his thoughts from his mind.

"We're here to have a conversation about it," he reminded her gently, stroking his thumb over that telltale vein. "So we might as well come to the point."

He hadn't meant to rekindle this spark with her, but it leaped to life of its own free will whenever they were near one another. It seemed foolish to pretend otherwise.

Her gaze lowered, settling on the place where their hands touched. "I think I had a different idea about what it would mean to settle our differences."

"Why don't you tell me what you hoped to accomplish today," he pressed. "You're not a woman who minces words either. So be honest with me. How do you suggest we go forward from here?"

She remained quiet for so long he wondered if she was going to answer. A breeze blew through the kitchen, stirring her red hair, a strand stroking along her cheek the way his hand longed to. When she lifted her chin, there was a determined glint in her eyes.

"With dogged resolve not to repeat the mistakes of the past."

He couldn't help but admire her, but he'd be damned if he was going to let her off the hook when he knew he wasn't the only one feeling tempted by what they'd once shared. "I couldn't agree more. But I can't say I ever viewed touching you or kissing you as a mistake. Far from it."

"That brand of thinking isn't going to solve the problem." She withdrew her hand from underneath his, but her restless gaze roamed over him in a way that eased the sting of rejection.

The caress of her eyes was far bolder than his hand had been.

"Neither is ignoring what we both want." He

folded his arms, daring her to contradict him. Craving the chance to prove her wrong.

Miranda didn't oppose him, however. "As temporarily satisfying as it might be to indulge ourselves, Kai, I think we have too much painful and complicated history for any good to come from falling into old patterns. We can't just pretend the hurtful parts didn't happen."

Had it been hurtful for her, too?

Her expression seemed to confirm it, but at the time, he'd viewed their breakup as one-sided. She'd moved on without him, turning her affections toward someone more successful. He'd thought he'd been doing her a favor by giving her up. The idea that there might have been more to it gnawed at him.

"You think renewing our affair is too risky." He summarized her point, winnowing it down to the bottom line. He paced away from her as he thought it over, his gaze shifting to the silent spill of water at the edge of the infinity pool on the patio.

"Yes." She sounded relieved that he seemed to understand.

But a good negotiator always had a backup plan.

"I disagree." He strode toward her again, liking the vision of her here, in his home. "We're both older and wiser. We wouldn't fall prey to the false illusions we had about one another ten years ago."

He stopped just short of her, his chest so close to her he could feel the heat radiating off her, the heat of their desire for each other. Except she looked ready to argue again.

"What about a compromise?" he suggested, before she could speak, still not touching her even though the ache for her was a tangible thing inside him.

She arched an auburn brow, questioning.

"One last kiss," he suggested, presenting his real agenda.

For now.

"I think that's a bad idea," she said quickly, reaching for her water glass again. She took a sip, then kept the cut crystal in one hand, a barrier between them.

Her lips glistened with moisture. His heart slugged faster.

"Is it?" He leaned closer, but didn't touch her. "Let me tell you why I think it's the best idea."

"Um." She shifted, her knee grazing his as she moved.

The brief feel of her stoked a fire inside him, but still he didn't touch her, needing her to make the decision. "It would let us end on a good note. Give closure to that chapter."

She set her glass on the counter, the tumbler clinking unsteadily on the granite. "I don't think so. And I'm not sure this is a fair discussion."

"Good debate calls for supporting arguments." He eased back enough to look into her eyes, a far deeper blue than the pool outside. "But if you're not interested in hearing how a kiss might clear away the thoughts that cloud my head when you're around—"

She closed her eyes for a moment, and he thought she was trying to shut down the conversation. But then she nodded. It was a gesture so slight it was almost imperceptible, but he'd seen it. Somehow that nod told him she was conceding the point. His pulse sped.

"If we're going to do this, make it count." Deliberately, she curved a palm around his neck and lowered his mouth toward hers.

She began by brushing her lips over his with a feather softness that made him groan.

Or maybe it was the feel of her luscious curves pressing into him that tore the sound from his throat. Either way, the sweet satisfaction of her hands on him, urgently gripping his shirtfront to draw him closer, was the best possible outcome.

Her lips parted, welcoming him, and he took his time savoring her, licking his way inside. He lingered in the places that made her breath hitch, remembering what she liked, reminding her what they could do to one another. He wrapped her in his arms, sealing her to him, positive no man could make her feel the way he could. The orange-jasmine scent of her skin fired through his senses while her fingers skimmed over his shoulders and down his back.

He tried telling himself it was just a kiss. That he couldn't handle any more than that. But the soft swell of her breasts against his chest, the shift of her hips muddled his thoughts. Her hips rocked, seeking, and he was lost.

The kiss went wild. Out of control. The needy sound she made in the back of her throat undid him. Her hands slid over his shirt and then her fingers made quick work of the buttons. She slipped one hand along the heated flesh of his bare chest, her nails lightly scoring. He forced himself back, knowing he needed to end this. Remembering she hadn't signed on for more than a kiss.

But before he could pull away completely, she captured his lower lip with hers, drawing on it in a move so sexy he had to grind his teeth together to keep from leaning her over the kitchen counter and pulling up her skirt.

"Miranda." He said her name, almost in a plea—needing her help if he was going to regain control.

Her blue eyes sprang open, but she didn't move away from him. Their heartbeats pounded wildly against his chest, and for a second, he couldn't have said which rhythm belonged to him. Need for her crowded out rational thought for long moments afterward.

Finally, her hands fell away from his chest.

He mourned the loss of her touch even as he said a prayer of thanks that he'd enlisted her aid. He'd never lost his head so fast for a woman.

Except with Miranda the first time.

Hell.

"I did warn you it was a bad idea," she reminded

him, stepping back enough to give them both some breathing room.

She combed restless fingers through her red hair and then gave her suit jacket a tug, straightening it. A bright emerald cocktail ring on one finger was a welcome reminder that she was no longer the ambitious waitress with dreams of a big future.

This Miranda was independent and successful, with a whole life waiting for her in New York. And she'd made it clear she didn't want to retread their past.

"We have very different ideas of bad." He was in no mood to argue now. Not until he had his head screwed back on straight. "Because what just happened there was so damned good it hurt. You know it was."

"You wanted a last kiss. You got it." She finished her seltzer water and walked over to deposit the glass in his sink. "Now we can close that chapter and focus on the bank's business."

He slanted her a sideways glance as he refastened a few of his shirt buttons. "You realize how ludicrous that sounds. I think it's safe to say I was dead wrong about a kiss settling the tension between us."

She peered out over the patio area, a warm breeze filtering in. Her cheeks were flushed pink, her lips softly swollen from his kiss. Huffing out a sigh, she turned back toward him.

"Until we figure out what that means, why don't

you show me the highlights of the house while we shake off the aftereffects?"

Her legs still felt shaky.

One kiss and she'd been ready to peel off all her clothes to relive the past with Kai. The rush of adrenaline must be what was making her skin buzz now. Maybe she should have just told him to take her back to her car.

But Miranda hadn't grown her business by being a quitter, and it bugged her to leave Kai's place without accomplishing what she'd come here for—to resolve the past so they could move forward with their professional partnership.

So even though the memory of the out-of-control kiss was still simmering in her veins, she followed him through his home, taking in the details of upcycled materials that had been used to achieve the sleekly modern aesthetic. Maybe her subconscious would tackle the problem of the kiss while she tracked the work Kai had done over the years.

She wasn't sure what impressed her most—the solar panels and collection of rainwater that made him far less dependent than most on conventional utilities, or the repurposed stone collected from teardowns around central Texas. He opened the last door on the bottom floor for her now, gesturing her inside a pale gray office space or lab of some kind, full of humming computers, a huge locked server cabinet and monitors everywhere.

"And this is my tech room," he announced, following her inside across the travertine floor. "I work on new software and gadgets in here. It's not so much an office as grown-up play space."

Her brain supplied a whole different set of visuals for a play space with Kai. She squeezed her legs together against the ache for him, but that only made it worse. Huffing out a pent-up breath, she focused on what she was seeing instead of what she felt.

"It looks a little high-tech for play," she observed, noting the electronic parts in various states of assembly at a counter along the far wall. There was a huge overhead lamp on one swing arm for easy movement, and a magnifying glass the size of a dinner plate on another.

"I come here when I get burned out on coding," he admitted, following her deeper into the room as if drawn forward by his favorite things. "I love my work, but when the thing you're passionate about becomes your primary means of income, it robs you of a good creative outlet."

Surprised by the keenness of the insight, she remembered another thing she'd enjoyed about Kai. No matter their other differences—his bad-boy ways that flirted with danger while she stayed firmly on the straight and narrow—they were both wired for high productivity and ambition. They'd been able to share their dreams and their passion for their work.

"I couldn't agree with you more." Walking through the space, Miranda recognized shades of the man she'd known. An artist's rendering of a futuristic-looking motorcycle hung on one wall. A framed photo of the groundbreaking for Madtec's headquarters rested on another. "I couldn't wait to share the peace I take from yoga with other people, and I get to do that in a big way with Goddess. But the business means I don't get to be in the studio as much I would like."

She felt his presence close to her shoulder, her whole body keyed in to his no matter how hard she tried to forget about that kiss in the kitchen.

He didn't linger by her, however. Instead, he moved toward the door as if ready to move on. He waited there for her. "We're lucky to have those kinds of problems. But I hope you make taking care of yourself a priority, too."

The simple sentiment lodged in her chest, touching her, affecting her as much as his touch. When was the last time someone in her life had urged her to put her wishes first? Even Buckley—a great champion of her ambition—had measured her success by her profit margin. Shaking off the draw of the old bond with Kai, it occurred to her that relating to him physically was a whole lot simpler than acknowledging the deeper chemistry.

"I try." She strode toward the door as he made way for her in the gray stone corridor.

He nodded. Leaned a shoulder into the doorframe as he considered her, his arms folded. "The only places left to show you on the tour involve…beds." His green eyes darkened. Even the word sounded silky on his lips. "Places I don't dare take you with the aftermath of that kiss still singeing my insides."

She did that to him?

Her gaze dipped to where the fabric of his gray dress shirt went taut around his biceps. Tendrils of desire teased her, tangling around her legs and rooting her feet to the floor.

Breathless at the thought of him needing restraint around her, she posed to him the question she couldn't answer herself. "What do *you* think we should do to fix this?" She hesitated. "To get us to a regular working relationship, that is."

"I wish I had a clear answer for that." Sincerity colored his words, leading her to believe he'd thought long and hard about it, too. "But all I know is that ignoring the attraction is only making it worse."

Her heart beat so hard it felt like her whole body pushed her inexorably toward him. Fighting what she wanted demanded all her energy. All her focus.

The memory of what it felt like to be in his arms roared through her. The seductive answer to her question seemed impossible to ignore when he stood so close to her, more appealing than any man she'd ever met.

"At least we agree on what's *not* working," she murmured, as much to herself as to him.

"Why don't you let me make you my priority for the rest of the day, Miranda?" he suggested, reaching out to skim a knuckle along her cheek.

The touch melted any argument she might have

made, any thought she might have had that didn't involve being with him.

Closing her eyes, she let herself focus on the place where his skin brushed over hers, the scent of him stirring her need while he continued to speak.

"We could step away from the problem of work for a while," he added, spinning a vision too enticing to resist. "And just…be."

Being with him would be so much more complicated than he was making it sound. But when was the last time she'd put what she'd wanted ahead of everything else? Her whole life had been about work and responsibility for years.

Opening her eyes, she found his.

"Yes." The affirmation of what she wanted felt like a step off a precipice, but it also felt damned good. She would take ownership of her choice. "I want to do more than see a room with a bed. I want to be in one. With you."

His knuckle stilled against her cheek as he seemed to absorb the words. Process them. And then, all at once, both hands cupped her face, lifting her chin for his kiss.

She stepped closer to him, wanting no space between them, needing Kai to deliver on the sensual promise he'd made. Now that she'd committed to this, she was going all in.

His mouth covered hers, claimed hers. His tongue stroked her lower lip, teasing a shiver that coursed through her whole body. She wrapped her arms around his neck, wanting to feel him everywhere.

He lifted her against him, his body a sensual friction against hers as her feet left the ground. She steadied herself with her hands on his shoulders while he turned them down a hall and up a stairway, his thighs stroking hers as he walked with her in his arms. His chest a warm weight against her breasts, his hips rolling against hers as they moved together.

Flames licked their way up her body, anticipation making her ready to come out of her skin by the time he shoved through a door into the master suite dominated by a platform bed with a padded leather headboard. He set her on her feet a moment before he leaned down to jab a remote. On cue, electronic blinds lowered to cover the windows while sconces flickered to life near a stone hearth on one wall, the low golden glow turning Kai's olive-colored skin to warm bronze.

The sight only fired her urge to see more of it. For the second time that day, her fingers went to work on his shirt buttons, desperate to feel him. Taste him.

"Miranda." Her name on his lips made her insides quiver. "I've missed your single-minded focus."

A startled laugh bubbled free, but it didn't come close to distracting her.

"You know how I am about goal setting," she teased, bending to kiss his sculpted pecs, his skin clean and his scent woodsy.

"And I enjoy being the focus of your goals." His

hands were steadier than hers, quickly undoing the jacket of her suit. "But I did promise to make you my priority, remember?"

The cool air of the room, stirred by an overhead fan, sent a pleasurable shiver through her before he flicked a bra strap off one shoulder. The emerald green silk tickled before he lowered a kiss to her collarbone.

She forgot everything else but how that felt, gladly giving herself over to his touch. His mouth. She'd tried to bury the memories of what it had been like to be with him, but the knowledge leaped to life now, adding to the anticipation coiling tighter inside her.

She lost track of how his skillful hands freed her from one piece of clothing after another, but her skirt slid down her hips even before her jacket fell away from her arms.

Kai edged back to look at her, his green eyes missing nothing while she tried to catch her breath.

"You're so incredibly beautiful," he informed her, shrugging out of his shirt. "It's unfair to other women."

Feminine pleasure danced through her at his over-the-top flattery. She toed off her high heels and then moved toward him, her bare feet silent on the cool stone floor.

"It's far more unfair that you get to see me, and I can't see you." Hooking a finger in his belt, she slid the leather through the buckle before unfastening his pants, his skin hot to the touch where her knuckle grazed his abs.

He bent to kiss her again, distracting her with a flick of his tongue. She wavered on her feet and he lifted her once more, turning to deposit her on his bed. The downy navy-and-white-striped duvet felt cool against her skin while Kai remained standing. She watched him strip off his socks and shoes before shedding his pants. His boxers.

Her throat went dry at the sight of him. At the reminder of how much he wanted her. A helpless, needy sound tore free from the back of her throat before she could stifle it. He covered her with all that warm, heavy muscle, and the pleasure of it nudged her closer to the edge of fulfillment. Every nerve ending vibrated. One strong thigh sank between hers and she gasped at the feel of it.

Her fingers flexed against his shoulders, drawing him down to her, but he wouldn't be hurried as he unfastened the front clasp of her bra. Sensation tingled and tightened, making her ache. He soothed it with his tongue, circling the tip of her breast, drawing on her until she pulsated with need between her legs.

That too he cared for, fingering her lightly at first, then harder, through the thin silk of her panties until she writhed for more. She was so close to finding release. So close.

Dimly, she thought of telling him. But before she could form words, his breath warmed her ear.

"Come for me," he urged her, the whisper of sound coinciding with a sweet, devastating stroke of his finger up the very center of her.

The orgasm spun through her like a whirlwind, seizing all of her and twisting pure pleasure from her. The sensations pulsed over and over, as if she hadn't found release in all the years since he'd last touched her. She gripped his wrist, holding him there, even though she knew she didn't need to. Somehow, he still understood her body so very well.

When her quivers subsided, he drew her panties down and off. Speechless still, she kissed him hard, pouring the feelings she couldn't name into passion. She felt him reach into the nightstand drawer and knew he returned with a condom. Not trusting her trembling hands, she let him take care of it.

Just the way he took care of her.

The thought captivated her for a moment as he slid inside her. Then, his green eyes met hers and she didn't think about anything but making him feel as good as he'd done for her.

Rolling him to his back, she rained kisses down his neck as she moved over him, rolling her hips into him. Softly at first. Then harder.

He wasn't the only one who remembered their old rhythms. She found the pace he liked as naturally as breathing. Desire built all over again. As if he hadn't just delivered a toe-curling climax for her moments before. Her hunger for him returned. Redoubled.

They moved in sync. Perfect. Blissful. Harmony.

Kai rolled her to her back, taking over with an urgency she recognized. The pleasure boiled over, seizing her once more, even harder than before. Only then did he let himself go, the shudder of his powerful body a testament to what he felt.

When he slumped to her side, dragging pillows under both of their heads and wrapping a quilt over their cooling bodies, he stroked her face and kissed her forehead.

He'd always been the most tender, caring lover she could imagine. And right now, he'd awakened feelings inside her that she couldn't begin to pick through with drowsy contentment weighing down her limbs.

"It's early yet," he said into her ear, skimming her hair away from her face. "You have a lot of hours of pleasure ahead before you're allowed to have any second thoughts."

It seemed he still knew how to make her melt with his words as much as his body, too.

"Ten years have made you a wiser man," she observed lightly, knowing she'd need to retreat to her own space before she could figure out what this time with Kai meant in the big scheme of things.

No sense overthinking it now when she was in a muddle.

"Ten years have made you sexier," he returned without missing a beat. "Do *Forbes* list executive women still like postsex backrubs?"

Already his fingers were trailing light circles around her shoulders.

"You know my weakness," she groaned, rolling over to give him better access.

For one night, she could indulge herself, couldn't she?

Closing her eyes, she promised herself she'd wade through the confusing questions in the morning. There would be time enough to figure out a way to work with Kai then so she could leave for New York with Blackwood Bank in good hands.

Too bad a little voice in the back of her mind told her that ten years hadn't made her one bit smarter when it came to resisting this man.

Six

As they pulled up to Natalie Valentine's bridal shop in downtown Royal later that week, Miranda asked the driver to give her a moment to refresh her makeup before she exited the car.

She should have done it on the way to the shop, but she'd been preoccupied with thoughts of Kai—the same way she had been pretty much every minute since the unforgettable night they'd spent together. So much for hoping that giving in to the attraction would help tame her runaway feelings.

With one hand, she raised the mirrored case of her eye shadow palette, and with the other, she swept powder over her nose. One of the perks of her role on *Secret Lives of NYC Ex-Wives* was having access to a makeup artist, and it had been kind of fun to sit back and let someone else do the work for the first few episodes, but as a woman with a lot of goals to tackle every day, Miranda soon found the time in the makeup chair felt excessively indulgent. As long as her face didn't shine and she had some mascara on her lashes, she was good enough. Why feed into the idea that women needed to spend hours on their makeup? Besides, she couldn't help but remember how nice it had felt to wash her face in the master suite at Kai's house the night they'd spent together and have him kiss every inch of her clean cheeks, swearing she'd grown lovelier in the last ten years.

She might have written it off as empty flattery except that his eyes had been sincere. His hands and mouth positively worshipful in their attention to every part of her...

Was it any wonder she couldn't keep her attention on something as mundane as what shade of lipstick matched her dress? Maybe time spent filming the show would help her corral her thoughts. She needed to tie up loose ends in Royal and head back to New York. Maybe it was just being back in Texas that had stirred all the old feelings for Kai. If that was the case, then leaving Royal should help her forget.

Satisfied she looked acceptable for the afternoon filming at the bridal shop, Miranda shoved the compact and makeup brush back in her bag and thanked the driver for waiting before she stepped out onto the sidewalk.

"Over here!" Seraphina called from beside the cameramen. She and Lulu looked like they were comparing shoes, their toes out like they were in ballet first position, their designer heels side by side.

"We're twinsies today," Lulu announced as Miranda got closer. "Fee bought the new Jimmy Choos in leopard print, and I snapped up the metallic silver."

"You'll set the new bridal trend for animal prints and glitter. I like it."

Lulu laughed, tossing her dark hair. "My wedding, my way, right?" She sounded more at peace with it since their talk earlier that week. "No sense going too conventional."

"Good for you." Miranda gave her a one-armed hug. She was thrilled for Lu, even if that meant being the tiniest bit envious. Who wouldn't want that kind of happiness in a marriage?

Miranda had tried marriage, putting all her considerable ambition and effort into making her union with Buckley a success, and it still hurt that it had been the biggest failure of her life.

A wicked smile curved Fee's lips. "You could do metallic cowgirl boots under your wedding dress and make all the bridesmaids match you. Rafaela would spontaneously combust at the thought."

Miranda relaxed into their chatter, soaking in the joy of being around her friends while they ramped up to the show's season finale. Rafaela and Zooey joined them a few minutes later and they took the wedding party into the bridal shop. Even Rafaela seemed impressed by Natalie Valentine, the knowledgeable shop owner whose inventory ranged from couture to vintage with plenty of interesting designers in between. Lulu spent a lot of time trying on international bridal gowns inspired by wedding traditions from around the world.

Miranda sipped champagne poured over fresh raspberries while she perched on a settee beside Zooey, watching Lulu twirl around in a beaded mermaid-style gown. The odd sense of envy nipped again, bugging Miranda, because she wanted to be a better friend than that to Lu.

Besides, it's not like Miranda believed she needed a man in her life to be complete. Far from it. If anything, she'd known greater contentment in her life since her divorce from Buckley, spending her time on friends and projects that were important to her. That fulfilled her spirit and nurtured her soul. So why the unrest now when her friend practically bubbled with joy?

Kai Maddox.

The man's face appeared in her mind's eye, distracting her all over again, assuring her that her mood today was entirely because of him. All at once, it occurred to her that some latent romantic part of her heart was craving something more with Kai.

It was a thought so startling she reared back from

the starry-eyed romanticism of it, nearly spilling her champagne. Only Zooey noticed.

"You don't like the dress?" Zooey started to ask after Lulu disappeared to try on the next gown. Zooey turned toward Miranda on the settee. As she saw Miranda's face, she frowned, her honey-colored hair dipping over one eye as she leaned closer. "What's wrong?"

One of the camera crew rolled closer to them. Maybe someone else had noticed Miranda's sudden unease.

Crap.

She could practically hear the camera zoom button whirring, knowing her face was coming into sharp focus. Any lie she attempted about would be dissected by viewers.

Knowing she wasn't ready to confide her thoughts about Kai to anyone, let alone their million viewers, Miranda trotted out the one other truth beneath her melancholy mood today and hoped it would be enough.

"It just feels like the end of an era, doesn't it?" She swallowed over the emotions causing a lump in her throat, focusing on the bubbles in her champagne. "Seraphina's staying in Texas with Clint. Lulu and Kace are tying the knot, and I'm betting they'll be here more often than New York, too."

Nearby, Rafaela and Fee were scrolling through their phones to read more about a bridal gown designer, though they looked up when they saw the second camera moving toward Miranda and Zooey.

"Like high school graduation," Zooey offered, the comparison making Miranda smile at the reminder of how young she was. "Happy and sad at the same time because things will never be quite the same. Plus, you know you'll never have the same amount of drama."

Maybe the high school comparison was more apt than she'd realized.

"Exactly like that," she admitted, her eyes lifting to include Fee and Rafaela as she set aside her drink. "I'm going to miss the girl time."

Lulu stepped out of the dressing room just then, wearing a simple white sheath dress that was understated enough to put all the focus on her. She stopped short on the pedestal, surrounded by mirrors and her bridesmaids, peering around at their faces.

"What did I miss?" she demanded. "Something good?"

"We're getting all sentimental about the wedding feeling like a last hurrah for us," Fee told her, hopping up on the raised platform to link arms with Lu before slanting a glance toward Rafaela. "Remembering that we like each other...most of the time."

Rafaela sniffed, but didn't argue, which was practically agreeing for her.

"I'm the *bride*," Lu reminded them, squeezing Fee's arm tighter. "You can't get sentimental without me. Save all gooey love talk for when I can be here to savor it."

Miranda set down her champagne and moved closer to the dressing platform, fluffing the bride's skirt. "This one gets my vote, Lu. You look amazing."

"I like this one, too." Zooey stood, smoothing a hand over her green floral minidress that made her hazel eyes more emerald. "But don't let Miranda deflect. She was all *verklempt* about this being the end of an era."

Rafaela sighed. "So does that mean we have to group hug? Because I just had a blowout and I don't want it crushed." She flipped her long dark hair over one shoulder as she came to her feet.

"Get up here, you ungrateful wench," Fee blustered, holding out a hand.

Miranda wasn't sure if Seraphina and Rafaela had made nice for the bride's sake, or if they were genuinely burying the hatchet, but she was glad for the peace among the group as they all joined the bride on her pedestal. The five of them looped arms around each other's shoulders, and she looked around at the other four faces of the women she'd plotted with, laughed with and cried with on more than one occasion.

"This is more like it," Miranda said. "If it's our last hurrah, ladies, let's make it a good one."

The cameras loomed, a boom mic hovering overhead, the intrusion oddly startling since she'd been so focused on her friends.

"We're going to rock this wedding," Fee added, squeezing Lu even closer.

"Do you think this is what guys talk about in their football huddles?" Zooey asked, narrowing her green eyes. "They look just like this when they're on the field."

"Except their asses are more fun to look at," Rafaela deadpanned.

Her phone buzzed in Miranda's pocket even though she'd set it to not disturb her. Very few contacts could override that and get a notification through. Excusing herself as she waved to her friends to continue the fitting, she moved to a quiet corridor just outside the dressing area of the bridal shop.

She was surprised to see a text from Kai on the screen.

Major security breach of Blackwood Bank data during transition to Madtec's new software. Need to see you ASAP.

A chill ran through her. Of all the ways she'd been fantasizing about seeing him again, this wasn't one of them.

"Vaughn." Miranda blurted her stepson's name, grateful to have gotten through to Buckley's son and the inheritor of the bank as she fastened her seat belt in the back of the town car. She'd already told the driver to head to Deer Springs. "We need to talk."

She'd left the bridal fitting immediately, knowing her friends understood the demands of running a business. And right now, she wasn't just in charge of Goddess. During the transition of the Blackwood assets to the rightful heir, she was still responsible. The weight of that felt heavy on her shoulders while she contemplated the possibility of exposing customer financial information to hackers.

"I've already heard about the breach," Vaughn informed her, his voice brusque. "From what I can tell, Dad's in-house security team has been running on fumes for too long. I can't say I'm surprised."

She stared out the window, focusing on her breathing to settle taut nerves as they hit the outskirts of Royal, the homes giving way to fields and farmland.

"I'm heading to Madtec now to assess the damage." She knew that hiring Kai had been the right move, but had it been too late to protect the bank's clients?

"Good. In the meantime, I'm going to have to call a press conference to get on top of this." Vaughn might have spent most of his life ranching, but he had the same good head for business as his father. "News like this leaks fast."

"Do you want me to be there for the press conference?" she offered, needing to make herself available to Vaughn. Kellan and Sophie had been the toughest of the Blackwood heirs to convince that she wasn't the step-monster they all once thought, but while Vaughn hadn't been as focused on fighting her and contesting the will, he'd been the most withdrawn of the siblings. In fact, he'd barely set foot in Royal over the past few months. It wasn't until he'd come back for Sophie's wedding and reunited with his sweetheart—and their surprise child—that he'd opened up to Miranda at all. Their relationship was friendly now, but still fragile, and Miranda wanted him to know that he could count on her.

"No," Vaughn answered quickly. "I'd rather have you at Madtec being our ears to the ground. Please loop me in on whatever measures they're taking to counterbalance this attack."

"Of course." She hesitated as her driver left Royal behind, heading south toward Deer Springs. And Kai. "I still feel sure that hiring Madtec was the way to go. The Maddox brothers are excellent at what they do."

There was a beat of silence before his reply.

"I'll admit their client list is impressive. But we're their first big financial customer, and they do have a hacking background—" Vaughn swore on the other end of the phone. "Look, Miranda, I'd better go. My public relations department is up to their ears in calls."

"We'll make this right," she assured him before disconnecting.

Grip tightening on her phone, she tried to gather her thoughts before seeing Kai.

She trusted him, despite the Maddox brothers' reputation as the bad boys of tech. She worried her lower lip, remembering how Kai had mentioned his regret over not giving Dane his full attention in the months before Dane to jail. She'd understood what he was saying. Kai been distracted wooing her.

No doubt Kai and Dane had something to prove.

Maybe she did, too. She might have failed at her marriage, but she would at least succeed in business. Blackwood Bank wasn't hers permanently, but she was in charge of it for now, and she would fight for this company to make sure it thrived.

She'd hired Kai because she believed he was the best. So if there was anything she could do to help him avert disaster, she was all in.

"Ms. Dupree to see you, Kai," Amad's voice came through a speaker in the on-site lab at Madtec.

"I'll be right out," he informed his assistant.

At any other time, Kai would have been glad to see her. But with the cybersecurity breach weighing on him like a lodestone, dread balled in his gut. This was no personal call. On this visit, Miranda represented Blackwood Bank, and the news from all sides was grim. He'd been pulled out of his bed at 5:00 a.m. on his day off to deal with the breach, alerted by Dane, who'd been on-site with one of the techs when the drama started to unfold.

Now, twelve hours later, Kai's eyes were beginning to cross from the stress and exhaustion of securing the site, assessing the damage and implementing a new system.

"I'll be back," he assured Jerrilyn, the systems engineer in charge of revamping the bank's cyber-security. "Call me if you find anything."

"We're fine," she assured him, never looking up from her screen. "We'll take care of this."

The hum of the electronic equipment and cooling fans was broken only by the occasional keystrokes of technicians scouring every inch of the breached site. In a lab of fifteen workstations, three computers were projected onto big screens so all the techs could track the progress of the new security data's installation, a slow process considering the massive undertaking. The initial installation had been interrupted by the breach, and they'd needed to do some cleanup on the site before they could try a second time.

Kai's gaze went to the central screen before he walked out to find Miranda. The new software would take all night to install, and that was running at the absolute fastest possible capacity. Madtec hadn't been prepared for this level of client demand so quickly into the relationship with Blackwood Bank, but at least—so far—the bank's internal tech team had taken the blame for the breach. They knew their security measures had gradually fallen apart before Madtec came on board.

But what would Miranda think?

It bugged Kai how much that mattered to him right now. After taking the elevator to his office, he walked past Amad's desk and into his office. Miranda's back was to him as she studied a photo on his bookshelves. No doubt she recognized the backdrop since it came from their long-ago trip to the beach in Galveston. The photo showed only his motorcycle, but the two helmets on the seat never failed to remind him of who'd been with him that day.

A silent reminder to him not to let himself get distracted again.

Miranda replaced the framed photo, her movement drawing his attention to the sweep of her blue chiffon dress sprigged with daisies. It was an ultra-feminine choice, reminding him he'd bothered her on the weekend when she'd no doubt been enjoying herself outside work. Memories of being with her at his place—never far from his mind this week—redoubled. For a moment, the urge to speak to her on a personal level, to pull her into his arms, was damn near overwhelming.

He ignored it, knowing his first loyalty had to be to his business.

"Thank you for coming." He shut the door behind them, ruthlessly reining in the need to touch her. "I'm sorry to interrupt your Saturday."

She turned, the hem of her dress swishing softly around her knees as her blue gaze locked on him.

"I'm grateful you phoned," she assured him,

shrugging off his apology. "The only reason I'm still in Royal is to oversee the distribution of the Blackwood assets. There is nothing more important to me than this."

While he appreciated her commitment to the project, the reminder where her loyalties lay still stung. But it was just as well to remember their reunion had happened only because of business.

He gestured to the high-backed leather chairs in front of his desk. "Please, have a seat, and I'll walk you through what's happening."

Miranda smoothed the full skirt of her dress before lowering herself into one of the chairs. Kai took the other, hitting a button on a remote to reveal a built-in projector screen on a wall between the bookshelves. When not in use, the black background broadcast a digital clock, but now it mirrored his laptop, where he had multiple tabs open to demonstrate the damage done by late-night hackers into the bank's system.

The frustration of seeing the bank's data compromised helped keep him focused on the task at hand instead of Miranda's nearness, her rapidly shifting sandaled foot the only indication of the tension she felt as he explained how many customers' financial data might have been compromised. No matter what life threw her way, the woman remained cool. Composed.

Always looking for her next move.

Throughout the briefing he gave her, she asked

few questions, but those she did were thoughtful insights, demonstrating her attentive eye for business. Not that he was surprised. She'd always excelled at extrapolating pertinent information, utilizing her resources to propel her work forward. Whether she was scouting locations for a yoga studio in downtown Royal the way she'd been doing when he first met her, or listening to a postmortem on a cybersecurity incident, Miranda could home in on the key points and carry forward a vision for her next move. That cool head of hers was always thinking, always working ten steps ahead so she didn't miss a thing.

All of which made her a formidable businesswoman, but it made her tough as hell to read on a personal level. And it made him wonder where the passionate woman who'd been in his bed earlier that week still lurked inside this self-possessed head of America's biggest fitness empire.

"So the hackers could have accessed financial data for up to ninety thousand customers." Miranda summarized the bottom line as she stared up at the projected screen. Then she turned to him. "How are we fixing that? What steps do we tell them to take, and what are we doing on our end to ensure it won't happen in the future?"

Tired from spending all day addressing the dumpster fire that was Blackwood Bank's cybersecurity, Kai knew he wasn't at his best. He couldn't restrain some frustration that she didn't seem rattled about the ninety thousand people who'd had their data exposed to fraudsters.

"For starters, tell the bank's customers they weren't being adequately protected by the last system, and that Madtec was brought into an impossible situation to try to fix it overnight," he pointed out, losing patience with the job, but also with Miranda's cool veneer that didn't reveal a hint of what they'd shared.

A frown pulled at her lips, and Kai rose out of his seat to stalk behind his desk, needing some distance from her.

"While I obviously can't do that, I realize this situation isn't of your making, Kai," she assured him, too damned reasonable to tell him he was being irrational and defensive.

Always a professional. And gorgeous. So desirable he ached to have her again.

He hauled his gaze away from the tempting sight of her and leaned a shoulder against the window looking out over a first-floor courtyard with the central fountain.

"The rest of the tech world won't be so gracious, I assure you." He ran a hand through his hair, blinking gritty eyes. "Madtec has put everything into steering our image away from our past, so a breach like this on one of our clients—our fault or not—is a huge setback if we can't get on top of this."

He needed to pull it together. The job. The meeting.

The desire for this woman who revealed so damned little of herself.

"You will," she said simply, rising from the leather armchair with the graceful movements that punctuated her every step. "I have every faith in you and Dane. But I can see you have your hands full with this situation right now. Should I leave you to do your job?"

How was it she could just shut down the attraction that still threatened to set him ablaze just looking at her? Nerves frayed and tension radiating through him—from work and personal things—he felt as overcharged as a live wire and yet exhausted at the same time. More than anything, he wanted to hold her, and the realization that he needed her with a tangible, physical hunger was more than a little daunting.

"No." He ground his teeth together to hold back words that might reveal the depth of that need.

When he didn't say anything else, she shifted her weight from one foot to the other, toned calves flexing. He thought he saw a hint of uncertainty in her eyes.

"Are you sure?" she asked, her manicured fingernails lightly resting on the black leather seatback, a bright blue cocktail ring winking in the slanting afternoon sunlight.

Something about her chiffon dress, so different from what she normally wore for work, gave him an idea. A way to appeal to her that might slip around those damned professional boundaries of hers.

"Actually, if it's just the same to you, the head of Blackwood Bank can leave." He straightened from his spot at the window, facing her head-on. "As for the woman I slept with? I'd like to speak to that Miranda right now."

Seven

A spark leaped between then, arcing in the quiet air of Kai's office.

Miranda exhaled as she stood next to his desk, some of the tension sighing from her lungs at his clear-cut directive.

She understood it. Empathized, even, because she felt the strain of reining in her feelings around him. No doubt he was exhausted. Stress and fatigue hung heavy on him, making her long to offer him some kind of comfort. But she could also see how dialed in he was to the task at hand. How engaged.

Leaving her leather bag on the back of the arm-chair, she circled the massive steel-and-wood work-station to face him, stopping just inches short of him.

"Speaking as the woman who slept with you," she began, threading her fingers through his because she couldn't resist touching him another moment, "you're seriously lacking imagination if you can't see past the bank executive to who I am underneath."

His green gaze darkened as he looked down at her. He shifted an inch closer, until there was just a hair's breadth of room between them.

"I can imagine every inch of the woman beneath. Vividly." His voice hit a gravelly note. "That may be part of the problem." He lifted their joined hands to his face and stroked the back of her fingers against his jaw. "But the other part of it is that you're the last person I want to let down right now, Miranda. Not because of the bank. Because of what's happening between us."

The honesty of those words sent a shiver of worry through her, because she didn't know where this relationship was headed either. Anxiety constricted her rib cage, a sharp confusion she still wasn't sure how to resolve. The uncertainty about Kai's expectations made it hard for her to simply enjoy the feel of him, even though she had an urge to lean into him, too.

She wasn't used to relying on anyone, and the neediness she felt scared her.

"Is there anything I can do to help…with the fallout from the cyberattack, I mean?" she asked, pulling her attention from his face to the big office around him, wary of falling into his arms while they were in the middle of a work crisis. If he noticed her dodging the subject, he didn't comment on it. "Vaughn is going to hold a press conference, but I told him I would update him once I knew more."

Unthreading their fingers, Kai stepped back, distancing them again. Her relief at sidestepping a thorny talk was overshadowed by disappointment at the loss of his touch. His expression shuttered, and she had the sinking feeling she'd disappointed him.

But she didn't know how to walk this line they were treading. She couldn't keep indulging a physical relationship when the business was her priority.

"Right." Kai nodded, moving past her to close his laptop. "In a perfect world, I would send someone to the press conference to represent Madtec, but unfortunately I need every available body on-site working on the Blackwood Bank problem." His gaze locked on hers, and there was no hint of the tender lover she remembered from their night together. "I've got to return to the tech lab to oversee things. Why don't you make yourself comfortable here, and I'll send up our PR rep to help you coordinate a statement from us for Vaughn. She can provide ideas for how to frame the news for your customers."

She bit her lip as she watched him retreat from her. Not just physically. She remembered how he'd withdrawn from her before they'd broken up ten years ago. It shouldn't hurt anymore, now that she'd stopped hungering for a romance to complete her.

And yet, the pang in her chest was undeniable.

"Kai—" she began, wanting to be more supportive of his work. Wondering if there was a middle ground for a relationship she wasn't seeing.

But he was already pushing through the double doors and out of his office. She glimpsed him leaning over his assistant's desk to give instructions before the heavy double doors swung shut again.

Later, she would figure out a way to make it up to him for not knowing how to be his lover in these circumstances. She was a better professional colleague anyhow. She wasn't leaving Madtec until she could see with her own eyes that the new security software was up and running. She would set up camp for the night in an office and provide whatever updates she received to Vaughn.

For now, she'd do what she did best. Take care of business.

"You should head home," Kai told his brother, Dane, eight hours later. "You look like roadkill."

Dane had just walked into the tech lab, his thick brown hair standing on end, his focus going straight to the overhead screen that broadcast the progress made on installing the new security software for Blackwood Bank. They'd wanted to test it further before rolling out the installation, but the breach had robbed them of that chance. They didn't have the luxury of time anymore.

Setting aside a fresh cup of black coffee, Kai swiveled in the ergonomic leather office chair at the center of the room, pushing back from his workstation. Three other systems analysts remained in the area with him, overseeing their own responsibilities in the implementation process, but the installation had all gone smoothly so far.

"You're just jealous you can't rock a beard like mine," Dane said absently, stroking a hand over the facial hair while he glanced at one of the other analysts' monitors on his way to the center of the room.

"Dude, you've been here so long there are probably small life forms setting up colonies in that thing," Kai returned, relaxing a bit at Dane's easy demeanor. It reinforced Kai's own sense that the crisis was abating.

If Dane was still worried about Blackwood Bank's system, he would be wired, no matter how little sleep he'd had. The zombie-like trudge of his brother's steps was reassuring as Dane reached the chair beside Kai's and lowered himself into it.

"Possibly. But if looking like roadkill keeps me out of the media, I'll take it." Dane tapped the screen to life at the workstation in front of him, refreshing a tab tracking the day's business news. "We're going to have to give in and get more aggressive about defending the Madtec image though, so someone will have to start speaking on behalf of the company."

A bad feeling crept up the back of his neck.

"What do you mean?" Kai asked.

"I mean we should have sent someone to the bank's press conference instead of just issuing a statement, because Vaughn Blackwood wasn't pre-

pared for the technical questions about the breach."
Dane hit a button to fast-forward a clip from the
local network news, stopping when it reached the
last third of the video.

The camera captured a weary-looking Vaughn
looking like a deer caught in the headlights as he
fielded detailed inquiries from journalists about the
nature of the breach, the party responsible and the
kinds of measures being taken to address the problem.
He kept returning to his note cards, reiterating talking points that only partially answered the questions.

"Shit," Kai muttered as he stared down at Dane's
screen, wondering if he should have encouraged Miranda to be there for the press conference. No doubt
she would have done a better job holding her own.
"I had our lone press relations expert working with
Miranda on the statement. That mistake is on me."

Before Dane could respond, the news coverage
swapped to footage of the Madtec headquarters,
where news vans were camped outside with a graphic
marked "Live" next to the images. A reporter told
viewers that they would obtain answers "as soon as
possible." Kai had no idea they were out there since
there were no windows in the tech lab at the center
of the building.

"The vans only arrived about an hour ago," Dane
informed him, switching off the tab to open a different program he'd been working on. "But since it's
after business hours, they haven't been able to enter."

"No one told me." Kai wondered if Miranda

knew. They'd exchanged a few texts over the last eight hours, but he hadn't gone back to his office since they'd parted ways. She'd settled in for the night, requesting periodic updates on the security installation, then feeding the information to Vaughn.

She'd refused to leave until Blackwood Bank was secured again.

Which Kai understood. But her rebuff had stung. Maybe it had been unfair of him to ask for his lover instead of his colleague though, given how important the fate of Blackwood Bank was to her. When she'd arrived, he'd already had hours to come to terms with the breach, but the news had still been fresh—and upsetting—for her.

"You might consider holding an impromptu meeting with the press of your own," Dane suggested, waving over an intern who'd just stepped into the tech lab with a fresh pot of coffee and a stack of cups.

Normally, they didn't allow food or drink in the lab, but the crisis of the big client breach had temporarily relaxed their standards.

Kai shook his head, even though he knew that meeting the media was inevitable. "No wonder you look like death warmed over," he observed wryly, understanding Dane wanted no part of the spotlight.

Grinning, Dane took a steaming cup from the local college student and set it carefully on his desk. "Method, meet madness."

Conceding the point, Kai was about to go up to his

office to speak to Miranda about it when the woman herself burst into the tech lab, her cell phone in hand.

"Kai, I'm so sorry to disturb you." She hurried over, walking so fast that her lightweight skirt sailed behind her a bit. Face pale, her features were drawn into a frown. "It's Sophie Blackwood. She's been rushed to the hospital."

Concern for Miranda, for her family, quickly shifted his focus.

"Why? Is she okay?" Kai was already on his feet, alert to Miranda's distress. He understood the importance of family.

"I don't know. Nigel just texted the family to let us know. They were just returning from their honeymoon and she fainted at the airport—"

"I'll take you," he told her shortly, steering her toward the door. He knew she hadn't gotten any more sleep than he had, so there was no way he was letting her go alone. He nodded to his brother, knowing Dane would oversee things. "Let's go."

Grateful for Kai's certainty about the decision, Miranda gladly let him lead her out a private entrance to the building. The warmth of his hand on the small of her back was a comfort even more than a pleasure, and she stayed close to him.

The last hours had been exhausting, monitoring the implementation of the new data security while exchanging calls with Vaughn about Madtec's progress. And then, there was the media interest and customer outcry. The media she didn't care about so much. But she was frustrated on behalf of the bank clients and wanted to do better for them.

Although none of that compared to her worries for Sophie. She'd just repaired her relationship with Buckley's only daughter. And while she'd never fooled herself that she could be a stand-in mother for the fiercely independent woman who was only a handful of years younger than her, she meant to be the most supportive friend possible.

"What about the news vans?" Miranda asked Kai as she stepped outside the building, peering in the dark to try to orient herself. "The press is camped out waiting to talk to you."

Long after midnight, the executive parking area was quiet, with only three vehicles visible.

"They're on the other side of the building," he assured her, pointing to their left where the glow of fluorescent streetlamps cast a bluish glow.

No sooner had they gone five steps than a spotlight popped on a few yards away from them, accompanied by the rush of footsteps and a rolling camera dolly. Miranda had been around enough of them to become intimately acquainted with the sound.

"Ms. Dupree!" a woman shouted as the sound of high heels pounded nearer, a camera eye winking to life beside her as a red light flashed a recording signal. "Is it true you chose Madtec to provide digital security because of your romantic involvement with Kai Maddox?"

Beside her, she felt Kai tense as he muttered under his breath. "I should have had security escort us. I don't know how they got through the fence." Then, holding up an arm to bar the camera's view of her, he continued to hustle her toward his car. "This is private property," he informed the camera crew. "You're trespassing, and there's no statement at this time."

"It's okay," she assured him, seeing their way blocked by a second duo of journalist and camera operator. She turned to speak into Kai's ear so as not to be overheard. "If we give them two minutes, they might leave. It might be faster than if we try to bulldoze through them."

His green eyes met hers, his face clearly visible in the bright wattage of the media lights as he seemed to decide whether or not to agree with her. Finally, he lowered his arm from where it had been shielding her face from view.

Miranda looked directly into the camera, knowing what she wanted to say after having spent hours working on potential statements with Vaughn. "Blackwood Bank has full confidence in Madtec. We are grateful to be the first financial institution to benefit from their new encryption software, and it couldn't have come at a more opportune moment."

"Will your relationship with the Madtec copresident be a storyline on *Secret Lives of NYC Ex-Wives*?" the woman asked, jarring Miranda since she didn't know how Kai felt about the show or his company's potential connection to it.

"No storyline is needed because there is no relationship," Kai shot back, spurring Miranda into motion again as he resumed a determined pace toward the silver Jaguar sports coupe. "No more questions."

The light and camera crews followed them, a second group joining the first in shouting provocative questions meant to incite a reaction. One of the women asked Kai if he hoped Miranda would move back to Royal, while another asked Miranda if Kai's "bad boy" reputation in the tech world had appealed to her. A man's voice wanted to know if Miranda's marriage had ended because of her previous relationship with Kai.

But by then, Kai had opened the passenger side door for her, and as she lowered herself into the seat, she saw two security officers dressed in Madtec uniforms rounding the building. No doubt they would ensure the journalists were relocated to the front parking lot where the other vans were.

Freed to move faster with the arrival of the guards, Kai pulled open the driver's side door and started the engine.

"That wasn't the business media, that's for damned sure," he observed darkly, driving quickly out the back gate and distancing them from the building.

"Probably tabloids. There are paparazzi down here following the show. I recognized one of the women from a seedy outlet that reports on celebrity scandals." She hugged herself, the run-in more disconcerting since it had happened with Kai at her side. And because the real story was supposed to be about Blackwood Bank, not a relationship between her and Kai.

Which, according to Kai, they didn't have anyhow.

His words harkened back to her now, along with the cold tone he'd used. No doubt he'd been irritated to be caught on camera in the first place, which she understood. Except she'd thought that he was angling for more of a relationship.

Wasn't he?

The silence between them stretched as he navigated through the vacant Deer Springs streets in the predawn hours, toward the highway to head north to Royal.

When he didn't speak, she glanced over at him. His jaw flexed, his mouth set in a flat line.

"I hope it wasn't a mistake to speak to the media. It didn't occur to me that anyone would ask about the show, or anything personal." Although even as she said it, she realized how naive she'd been to think she could keep her personal life separate from the Blackwood Bank trouble. "I should have anticipated it, however."

He seemed to weigh her words before answering carefully, "For someone as determined as you are to keep your professional image at the forefront at all times, I'm surprised you decided to do that show in the first place."

The highway unfurled before them in an endless-seeming gray path outlined in yellow and white. No other cars were on the road, the farms dark and silent on either side of them. Inside the luxury sports vehicle, the dashboard lights were minimal, highlighting the angles of Kai's handsome face.

Miranda wasn't sure if she should be offended about his implication that the show was the opposite of "professional." She supposed she could understand why he'd feel that way.

"The show may be over-the-top, but the relationships are real. And viewers relate to seeing how we handle crises of friendship." She remembered the young woman on the stairwell in the Madtec building who'd asked for her autograph. "I think we give women hope that life can be rewarding and fulfilling even if romance doesn't work out. We have plenty of things to be passion about. And we have each other."

"From the promos, it looks more like the show is about catfights and competitive shopping." He adjusted the air conditioner, and she felt the chilly breeze around her legs subside.

A different kind of coolness ran through her at his words, though.

"Marketing hooks don't always reflect the substance of a product," she retorted, miffed at the way people could write off feminine art. And yes, what they created was a kind of art, even if she was too tired to march out that particular argument tonight. "That doesn't mean the substance isn't there."

"Fine." His words were clipped as he acknowledged the point. "I was just curious why you did the show. Now I know."

"I hated failing at my marriage, that's why," she told him honestly, too irritated and out of sorts to hold back the way she normally would. "*Secret Lives* shows another side of life for women. Not just their dating. But their businesses. Their friendships."

Frustration simmered as she remembered the way Kai had denied they had a relationship. Even though she'd been the one to ensure that new boundaries went up between them since their night together, his slight had still hurt tonight. She told herself it was probably because she was also worried about Sophie. She hadn't heard any updates since that first text from Nigel.

"Then it's a good thing I told that reporter we don't have a relationship," Kai mused as they saw a sign for the exit for Royal. "Since it's clear you don't plan on having one."

She couldn't argue with that.

She'd thought as much herself, hadn't she?

And yet, as they drew closer to Royal Memorial Hospital, Miranda couldn't deny that she'd thought about Kai—and romance—every moment since she'd left his house earlier that week. The idea that he didn't see it as the start of a relationship caused an ache in her chest to deepen, and she didn't have a clue how to make the hurt stop.

Eight

An hour later, Miranda sat on the edge of the creaky vinyl chair in the emergency room waiting area, checking her phone for updates on a business meeting she needed to delay with AMuse, a rival fitness chain. When she'd agreed to the meeting, she'd hoped to be back in New York next week, but between the Blackwood Bank crisis, the Royal Gives Back gala she still needed to plan, Lulu's wedding and not knowing what was wrong with Sophie, Miranda didn't think the timing would work out.

She would just have to juggle things as best she could from here, delegating as much as possible to her staff while she waited for news about Sophie. Just as she started typing a message to her assistant to reschedule, Kai strode back into the waiting area. And how was it that even when she should be engrossed in work, she felt his presence? A cup of coffee in each hand, he dodged a toddler pushing a truck around the floor while the boy's grandmother read a paperback. That was all the action in the waiting room right now, since it was three in the morning. Vaughn had fallen asleep after the press conference, so she'd been unable to reach him. Kellan and Darius were both out of town, but she'd spoken to them both briefly to let them know about Sophie. Kellan hadn't wanted to wake Irina at this hour unless it was an emergency, but he'd promised to call her once the sun rose so she could be with Sophie either way. An ambulance had rushed in someone earlier, but there'd been no family with the older man.

How much longer until Nigel appeared with an update about Sophie fainting?

"Thank you." She took the cup Kai offered her, then met his weary green eyes. "You must be running on fumes."

"I'll sleep soon enough." He took the seat beside her, winking at the adventurous toddler who was slaloming his truck between chair legs now. "Dane said the download just finished. He's going to work for another hour and then he'll crash, too. We're in good shape."

Testing her coffee, Miranda tasted the soy milk she preferred. "Yum. You've got a good memory, Kai Maddox. Thank you."

How strange that something so small could make a person feel so well cared for.

"We shared enough breakfasts that I ought to remember," Kai said before he tried his own drink.

A nurse peered into the waiting room and then hurried back out, calling something to an orderly with a wheelchair. The loudspeaker squawked, paging a doctor. All normal activity.

Except life was far from normal for her right now.

Miranda's attention returned to Kai as she mulled over his words. "I shared more than a few meals with Buck, but he wouldn't have known my favorite color or song, let alone how I like my coffee."

"Green. And Sinatra's version of 'Summer Wind.' Or at least, it used to be." Kai pulled her favorites from his brain as easily as if he were citing multiplication table facts. "I never did understand what you saw in Blackwood beyond his money."

The warmth she'd been feeling toward him dissipated. Defensiveness prickled and she was tempted to snap at him, but another nurse appeared in the waiting room. Miranda's heart stuttered in anticipation. Kai shot to his feet. But the nurse waved over the grandmother and little boy. Leaving Miranda and Kai alone.

He sank back into his chair with a lengthy exhale.

"It was never about his money." She set aside her coffee, wishing Nigel would make an appearance soon and tell them what was going on with Sophie. "How could you think that? I married Buck because

I thought our goals and interests were aligned. On paper, we made good, practical sense. He encouraged my business ideas. I helped him grow his empire. I thought we'd be a good team."

Kai shook his head before slanting her a sideways glance. "And you and I didn't make sense?"

His tone was challenging. But then they'd never cut each other any slack before. Why should now be different?

Did she *want* it to be different?

"We were passionate, not practical." She'd been happy with passion at first, but then she'd believed the passion must have been fading—on his side, at least—when Kai had withdrawn from her. She'd been devastated. Brokenhearted. Not that she'd ever confess the depth of that hurt to him.

"We were lovers and friends, too," he reminded her, his dark eyebrows furrowed. Clearly her view of the past didn't line up with his. "We had both."

Old regrets tugged at her, but she hadn't made the decision to end things lightly.

"You might have been enthusiastic about my ideas for Goddess, but you were more wrapped up in your coding world than anything." She smoothed the wrinkles from her filmy skirt. "I think you saw me as an escape from work, whereas I wanted to share my professional journey with you, and I wanted to know more about yours, too."

"You wanted a business partner?" he asked drily, stretching his arm along the back of her chair, his hand grazing her shoulder. "Being lovers and friends wasn't enough to get the job done?"

Had she expected too much from their relationship? Maybe. She'd been so in love with Kai, there was a chance she'd lost herself with him a little. Lost her bearings. Passion was exciting and heady, but it could be overwhelming, too. The realization—and the worry that she might have subconsciously pushed him away because of it—robbed her of a reply.

Just then, the double doors to the patient rooms opened, and Sophie Blackwood's new husband, Nigel Townshend, walked through them. Though he was impeccably dressed as always, the Green Room Media studio executive's expression appeared tired and—happy?

"Miranda." He gave her a slight smile as he caught sight of her and headed their way. The normally unflappable Brit looked decidedly worse for wear in his wrinkled suit. His tie was gone and his hair stood on end as if he'd raked fingers through it a few too many times. "Thank you for coming."

"How's Sophie?" she asked, coming to her feet. Then, as Kai rose beside her, she introduced the two men. "Nigel, this is Kai Maddox. Kai, Nigel Townshend works for the studio that produces *Secret Lives*."

The two men shook hands briefly, nodding acknowledgment. Then Nigel spoke.

"Turns out Sophie's fine," he explained, his blue eyes still a bit dazed. "The doctor thinks she got dehydrated because she's pregnant—"

Miranda drew in a breath, ready to celebrate the news, when Nigel finished his sentence.

"—with twins."

The news left her stunned, but overjoyed at the good news. Relief streaking through her that Sophie was all right, Miranda hugged Nigel, then turned to hug Kai without thinking—only to stop short. "That's wonderful news."

Kai cleared his throat and agreed, "Yes, it most certainly is." He shook the father-to-be's hand again. "Congratulations, man."

"Thank you," Nigel said with genuine joy. "I couldn't be happier. Although I really do need to return to my wife so we can process the big news together."

"You're sure you don't need us to do anything for you, Nigel?" Miranda asked, ticking through the possibilities in her mind. "You came here straight from the airport. Do you need food? Or should we stop by your house and get Sophie some clothes?"

"The doctor isn't admitting her." Nigel ran a hand through his light brown hair, his Patek Philippe watch glinting in the fluorescent lighting. "We're just getting a referral to be sure she can see an obstetrician tomorrow, and then I'll take her home."

A silence took hold in the wake of Nigel's departure, leaving her standing alone with Kai. Clearing his throat, he gestured toward the door.

"Should we go?" he asked, startling her from her thoughts of babies and marriage. New beginnings.

"Of course." She nodded, happy for Sophie even as she wondered what kind of relationship she would have with the Blackwood family once she left Royal.

She wanted to meet the twins. More than that, she wanted to hold them. Be a part of their lives.

She blinked past the rush of feelings, telling herself she was just tired.

Leaving the hospital together, Miranda saw the sun was just rising as they reached Kai's silver sports car.

"I'm thrilled for Nigel and Sophie, but I've lost all track of time," she murmured, exhaustion kicking in now that she didn't have worry and stress driving her forward. And yet Kai had been awake for longer. She couldn't let him drive all the way back to Deer Springs. "I can't imagine how you're still coherent."

"I'll be fine. And I'll have you home soon," he promised, holding the door for her as she took her seat and buckled up.

Her eyes followed his broad-shouldered frame as he strode around to the driver's side, her hungry gaze tempered by the realizations in the hospital waiting room.

Had she given up on passion prematurely when she broke things off with Kai? Yes, he'd pushed her away, but now she knew why. Her mother had been moving him around like a chess piece to ensure Miranda ended up with Buckley. Miranda could have found that out back ten years ago—but she hadn't asked. She'd felt Kai stepping back, and she'd just let him go.

It was difficult to accept that what she had with Kai was well and truly over when she still felt so drawn to him.

As he settled into the driver's seat and started the car, she watched his movements. She could see the flex of his forearms where his shirtsleeve remained rolled up from working. His broad, capable hands wrapped around the steering wheel, and she was transfixed by the memory of what his touch did to her.

He caught her staring.

"I'm curious what you're thinking right now." He didn't put the car into gear, his gaze wandering over her.

That simple attention stirred her insides, her nerve endings flickering to life.

"It occurred to me that you can't possibly drive back home tonight. You can stay at the guesthouse." She would have made the offer even if she hadn't been genuinely concerned for his safety. There were no two ways about it. She wanted Kai in her bed. "With me," she added, her voice grazing over a husky note.

Desire darkened his eyes. She shivered from the awareness tickling over her skin.

"And just like that," Kai spoke softly as he put the car into gear, "I'm not the least bit tired."

Fifteen minutes later, Kai held Miranda snugly against his side, nuzzling her neck as she entered the security code on the guesthouse.

A night breeze blew through the filmy skirt of her dress, lifting the fabric enough to brush his pant leg. A touch so subtle he shouldn't have been able to feel it, except that his nerve endings were wound tight, his senses keenly attuned to this woman.

The scent of her shampoo mingled with the light fragrance she wore that smelled like jasmine. Her red lacquered fingernail hovered over the buttons on the security panel, as if she was unsure what to press next. He wondered if she was distracted by the same fire in the blood that roared inside him.

While she searched for the next numeral to input, Kai bent closer to taste the skin exposed along the back of her neck. A breathy sigh erupted from her lips, her head tipping toward him as she leaned into the kiss.

As much as he couldn't wait to explore the rest of her, to indulge himself in her sweet responsiveness, he also knew they needed to be inside the house for what he had in mind.

"Did you forget the code?" he asked, sliding a hand around her waist as he kissed his way to the hollow beneath her ear.

"No." She hit another number and he skimmed his touch higher, brushing the underside of her breast. With a sharp intake of air, she jabbed the last number hard. "Just distracted."

The alarm chimed an agreeable tone, allowing her to open the door and step away ahead of him. He followed her inside, trying not to think about the fact that this place once belonged to Buckley Blackwood, the man who'd stolen Miranda from him.

The man he'd believed Miranda wanted more than him.

Thoughts of the man stilled Kai. Tonight, he'd learned that she hadn't been wooed by his wealth. Yet ten years ago, Kai had been quick to believe the worst of her, probably because of his own insecurity about the hardscrabble kind of life he would have been able to give Miranda back then. He'd given her up too easily.

A mistake he wouldn't repeat.

Miranda called to him from the kitchen while he still stood in the entryway. "Can I get you a drink? Something to eat?"

The sound of her voice spurred him back into motion.

"No. Thank you." He followed her into the kitchen where he'd brought her pie from the Deer Springs Diner.

She was already at the island, a hip leaning against the white quartz countertop, pouring two glasses of water from a green bottle before returning it to the refrigerator. Kai paused by the island long enough to tip the beverage to his lips, his eyes following her movements as she ran a hand through her gorgeous red hair.

"I'm not hungry either," she agreed, joining him at the counter to pick up her glass for a sip of the sparkling water.

"Who said anything about not being hungry?" he asked, setting aside his drink before he bracketed her hips in his hands. He walked his fingers down her thighs, lifting the fabric of her skirt as he moved, baring more of her legs to his gaze. "I'm starving for a taste of you."

A stillness took hold of her as her blue eyes locked on him while he rucked up the skirt. Then, lowering her glass, she steadied herself with her hands on his shoulders. He traced the lace fabric of her panties with his finger while she sucked in a gasp.

His temperature spiked. And then their hands were all over each other, roaming and exploring. She smoothed a touch over his chest and shoulders. He pressed his palm between her legs and her hips arched into him. He kissed her deeply, liking the small sounds of pleasure that hummed in the back of her throat. He was so damned greedy for her, he all but forgot where they were. When she stepped back, it took him a moment to blink through the hunger for her and remember they were standing in the kitchen.

She drew him forward by the hand, and he recovered his wits enough to follow the hypnotic sway of her hips as she moved down a lengthy hall toward a bedroom. He could see the king-size platform bed through an open door. A gray coverlet that looked like crushed velvet beckoned.

As they crossed the threshold, the scent of fresh flowers wafted from the nightstand where a vase of coral honeysuckle and daylilies rested. Behind the bed, a black-and-white print of downtown Houston took up a whole wall. But these were details he only half noticed as Miranda peeled down the top half of her dress, letting the silky fabric fall to her waist. A statement clear as a gauntlet dropped, and he'd be damned if he'd leave it unanswered.

Stress from the last twenty-four hours evaporated. All thoughts and doubts faded. The only thing he felt now was hunger for her.

"Let me help," he insisted, reaching for the buttons on her skirt. "I want to feel you as I undress you."

"I'd like that." She shifted her fingers to his shirt, working her way down the placket. "I want to feel you, too." She rolled her hips in a way that shifted her thighs against his. "All of you."

His body responded instantly.

"Happy to oblige." He tugged her dress down and off, leaving her in just a whisper of silk and lace that shielded her from view.

He shrugged out of his shirt as soon as she undid the final button, then shed his pants, socks and shoes, tossing them in easy reach of the bed.

Her eyes followed his movements, locking on his body in a way that was damned flattering. And burned away his last reserves of patience.

Lifting her against him, he carried her to the bed and laid her down in the center. Taking only a moment to admire how beautiful she looked with her fiery-red hair in the center of the gray velvet, Kai fell on her like a starving man. He kissed his way down her neck to her breasts, nipping and licking her through the thin silk barrier of her bra. She wriggled out of one strap and then the other, tugging the cups lower to give him full access. Gladly, he savored her bare skin, finding the source of her jasmine scent in the valley between her breasts. When he kissed his way lower, he dragged her lace panties down with his teeth, listening to every nuance of her breathing as he touched the sweet, hot center of her.

He glanced up for a glimpse of her face. The flush spreading across her chest told him she was so close to release already, as on fire for him as he was for her. He licked her and kissed her, loving the taste of her. Her release hit suddenly, surprising him with how quickly she flew apart in his arms.

A few hammering heartbeats later, he took his time retrieving his pants where he'd tucked a condom in his wallet, needing a moment to regain his self-control. But Miranda took over the task, ripping open the packet and sheathing him with eager hands.

Which totally worked for him.

Everything about her turned him on. Turned him inside out. When she reversed their positions, she climbed on top of him to straddle him. His breath came in a harsh rush, his heart slamming hard against his chest. He looked up at her in all her feminine glory and forgot everything else but being inside her.

And then he was.

Moving slowly at first, and then faster. She raked her nails lightly down his chest, a welcome counterpoint to the feelings that threatened to send him hurtling over the edge too soon. He rolled with her, putting her on her back so he could enjoy her that way, too.

"You feel so good, Kai," she murmured, her eyes half closed as she writhed beneath him.

It might have been the movement or her words, but something about the moment sent him hurtling toward completion long before he wanted. The realization slammed into him that he hadn't brought her to that precipice with him, yet at the same moment, her legs wrapped around his waist, and she found her own release with him. Fulfillment rocked him even as he acknowledged how thoroughly she made him lose control.

As the sensations continued to ripple through him, Kai couldn't remember the last time he'd been so consumed by passion. Probably, it had been with Miranda ten years ago.

Sliding to the side of her, he felt a wave of tenderness for the woman in his arms. A feeling he had no business having for Miranda given how soon she'd be out of his life again. But he ignored that thought as he wrapped her in the soft coverlet and tucked a pillow under her tangled red hair, thinking she'd never looked more appealing to him.

Emotions crowded his chest, but he pushed them aside for now and simply kissed her on her forehead.

She had to be tired. And he was, too. He hoped that was why he felt the urge to invite her to Deer Springs and spend more time pursuing a relationship. He knew that would never work since she had a whole life away from him in New York.

He shouldn't trust her anyway, based on how fast she'd put him out of her life the first time.

They didn't make sense on paper, she said.

And no matter how much he might wish it otherwise, they still didn't.

Nine

Miranda paced the floor of the guesthouse office the next morning after slipping from the bed she'd shared with Kai. She hadn't wanted to wake him, knowing his sleep deficit had far surpassed hers when they'd finally dozed off. She'd done her morning yoga poses out in the detached studio, then she'd returned to the office where a pewter pitcher full of purple coneflowers and sunflowers rested on the narrow secretary desk by her laptop. She carried a mug of mint tea to the desk and took a seat, hoping to use this time to somehow untwine her messy knot of feelings for the man sleeping just a few rooms away.

She'd told herself that she could resist his charm enough to prevent herself from falling for him again, but the more time she spent with him, the more she wondered if that was possible. History seemed to be repeating itself. And with that thought, she realized it might help to call her mother.

A crazy idea, maybe, she acknowledged as she pulled out her cell phone and scrolled through her contacts.

But the need to reconnect with her mom—to confront her about interfering in Miranda's relationship with Kai ten years ago—had preyed on her mind ever since Kai had revealed the role Ginny had played.

Leaning back in the leather office chair, Miranda tried to breathe through her nervousness as the call rang. And rang. She was about to hang up when her mother's voice sounded in her ear.

"Hello?"

Even from that lone word, Miranda could hear the husky rasp of exhaustion in her mother's tone.

"Hi, Mama. It's Miranda. Did I wake you?"

"Miranda?" Shuffling noises sounded on the other end of the call. A brief coughing spell ensued before her mother returned. "I'm surprised to hear from you."

Guilt pinched, but not for long. They hadn't parted on good terms the last time they'd spoken.

"How are you feeling?" she asked, knowing her mother always had a litany of health complaints—and yet her mother's ailments only increased the more "medicine" she took. The prescription pill problem ebbed and flowed over the last fifteen years, compounded by Ginny's refusal to get help.

"Since when do you care how I feel?" Her mother's words came wrapped around a cigarette, spoken out of one corner of her mouth. Miranda knew her mother so well, the small distortions of her words familiar to her after living with her for over twenty years. The flick of a lighter sounded, then a long exhale. "I seem to recall you didn't want me anywhere near you the last time I came for a visit."

Defensiveness pricked along her skin.

Ginny had arrived on the set of *Secret Lives of NYC Ex-Wives* during the first season, determined to be a part of the show. Miranda had refused. She had enough trouble navigating a relationship with her mom privately, let alone having the bond subject to public scrutiny.

"I would have been happy to spend time with you," she reminded her, glancing over her shoulder to ensure the door to her office remained closed. She didn't want to wake Kai. "But I got the idea you were only interested in visiting if our time together was televised."

Ginny sniffed. "I forgot you only show the world your cleaned-up side."

Miranda clutched her mug of tea, inhaling the minty scent and focusing on her breathing to ease the sting of the gibe that hurt more than she would have expected, maybe because there was some truth in it. But she'd worked hard to become the person she wanted to be. Why should she have to dwell on the unhappy pieces of her past that refused to heal?

Her mom had chosen her path—and continued to choose it, over and over again. Speaking of which, Miranda had a question to ask, and hedging only increased the nervous tension.

"Do you remember me dating Kai Maddox? Back when I still lived at home?" She'd remained in Deer Springs well into her twenties, determined to help her mother get clean.

It took a long time for her to learn that no one could help an addict who wouldn't help herself.

"The motorcycle guy who was too young for you?" Another puff on her cigarette, the exhale a long, protracted sigh. "Sure I do."

Closing her eyes against the wave of frustration she felt, Miranda traced the rim of the stoneware mug with her fingertip.

"I never thought he was too young for me," she reminded herself more than her mom. Only six years separated them, a difference no one would blink at if the older party happened to be male. "And I cared for him a great deal." She'd loved him. "Do you remember why things didn't work out for us?"

Her mother snorted dismissively. "Seriously? Buckley Blackwood and his millions came calling, Miranda. No one would blame you for having your head turned."

Clinging to her own memories of the past, Miranda felt sure that hadn't been the way it had happened. Buckley had liked her from the first—that much was true. He'd come to her yoga studio not long after his divorce from his first wife, Donna-Leigh Westbrook. He'd immediately asked Miranda out, but she'd declined. Unperturbed, he'd continued to take classes with her. He'd sent flowers. He'd been a gentleman, but he'd also been persistent, sending her invitations to exclusive local events and introducing her to a few key members of the Texas Cattleman's Club who'd been instrumental in building her business.

But she'd been in love with Kai.

"My head wasn't turned by his wealth." She couldn't swallow back the defensiveness, remembering how careful she had always been to make sure the world knew she hadn't married him for his money. "I signed a prenup, remember? When we divorced, I walked away with nothing." She'd been determined to prove to the world she could make it on her own after her marriage fell apart, and she had. But she hadn't phoned her mother to talk about that. With an effort, she breathed through the simmering resentment and asked, "What I want to know is did you say something to Kai to send him away? To make him think I cared about Buckley and not him?"

As soon as she asked the question, she regretted it. She knew Kai wouldn't lie to her about something like that. Yet it upset her to think her mom had quietly upended Miranda's life like that without her knowing.

Her fingernails bit into her palm.

"That was a long time ago," Ginny informed her after a long pause. "I don't think I ever had much to say to the motorcycle-riding boyfriend."

This was a mistake. Closing her eyes, Miranda heard sounds emanating from the kitchen and inhaled the scent of frying bacon. She grappled for a way to end the phone call that was only frustrating her and not providing any answers. She dragged in a breath, but her mother spoke again before she could get a word out.

"Although now that you mention it," Ginny continued, "there was one time when he stopped by just as the floral delivery truck left. He asked me about the huge arrangement, and I remember being frank with him about Buckley having his eye on you. Why all the interest in Kai now?"

Miranda needed to end the call. With the hint of fresh coffee wafting in the air, she knew Kai was awake. She just hoped she could still enjoy their time together now that talking to her mother had her tense and stressed all over again.

"No reason," she lied, feeling twitchy and anxious. "I'll call again soon, Mama."

Disconnecting the call, Miranda tried to shake off the knowledge that her mother had poisoned her relationship with Kai ten years ago. Understanding the role she'd played helped her to forgive—a little bit anyway—Kai's withdrawal. Now, anticipation curled through her belly and it didn't have anything to do with the food. Being around him made her feel like a twenty-something again, full of starry-eyed romantic notions that she knew better than to believe.

Didn't she?

As she padded barefoot toward the kitchen, she really questioned how much she'd learned from her previous relationships. She knew she shouldn't count on something as fleeting as passion, and she couldn't expect any man to be a full-fledged partner in her life. Yet with Kai, she found she was wrestling back the persistent beast of hopefulness all the time.

The thought gave her pause, slowing her steps just as she reached the archway leading into the kitchen. Was it too late to retreat?

"Good morning," Kai greeted her, making any attempts to escape a moot point. "I hope you're hungry."

Hungry? Absolutely. For more than food. The enticing man standing at the stove was most definitely a feast for her eyes as he carefully flipped an omelet in one frying pan while monitoring a second omelet and bacon in another. He wore his jeans and a black unisex T-shirt emblazoned with the Goddess fitness logo that she'd left out for him the night before. With his hair damp from his shower and his face unshaven, he looked clean and roguish, like a man who would taste delicious.

Shivery sensations tripped over her skin thinking about what they'd shared the night before. And not just in a physical sense. His presence at the hospital, his insistence on driving her there to check on Sophie, touched her. Finding him in the kitchen, making them both breakfast, reminded her of when they'd been a couple.

"It smells great. How can I help?" She was already moving toward the coffeemaker, pulling mugs out of the cupboard and wondering how she was going to find her equilibrium with him today.

She might be tempted to lean into his warmth and support as a lover and a friend, but where would that leave her if he pulled away from her again? Her mother may have played a role in their relationship's demise, but Kai had never let Miranda weigh in on that conversation either.

She needed to be careful.

"Just butter the toast and we'll be good to go." He slid crispy slices of bacon onto two plates, each decorated with an orange slice. Fresh juice was already poured in glasses on the kitchen table. "Have you been awake long? I saw you were on a call before I started breakfast."

After taking care of the toast, Miranda poured two cups of coffee, finding it far too easy to fall into their old rhythms of working together. Had she been wrong to write off what they'd shared as purely passionate and therefore impractical?

"I woke up about an hour ago and felt like I should touch base with my...office." That much was true as she'd checked in with her assistant at Goddess before she'd called her mom. But she wasn't ready to share about her uneasy conversation with Ginny. Instead, Miranda carried the mugs to the table, noticing Kai had already put the creamer she preferred beside her place setting. "I've been in Royal for so long. I feel guilty about leaving my staff, but they've handled what they can really well."

He brought over their plates. "That sounds to me like there are tasks you haven't given them to manage. Are there things you need to be there for personally?"

He held her chair for her, silently inviting her to sit. She told herself to relax and enjoy Kai's attentiveness while it lasted.

"I need to meet with my biggest competitor, AMuse." Settling into her chair, she laid her napkin in her lap while he took the seat across from her. Their knees bumped and the jolt of electricity had her skin tingling. "Their CEO has called twice in the last month and I'm curious what that's about."

"Do you think they might try to buy you out?" He sipped his black coffee, his green gaze finding hers over the rim of the stoneware mug.

"I wouldn't think so, but either way, I'd never sell." She had to look away from his assessing eyes, unsure where she stood with him today or what the night before had meant for him. Instead, she thought back to the early beginnings of her business and how hard she'd worked to grow it. "Building Goddess helped me find my own strength. Every setback taught me something."

"I feel the same way about Madtec." He pulled out his phone between bites of the omelet and tapped a few buttons on the screen. "I double-checked with my pilot—the Madtec jet is available. We could be in New York before the close of day. Why don't we go check on things at Goddess and put your mind at ease?"

The suggestion caught her off guard.

"Really?" While her own business was thriving, she had never had the need for a jet or regular pilot service, but she could certainly see the appeal. "What about the bank? Should we be overseeing anything more with the hacking incident?"

Nibbling on a bacon slice, she ran through a mental checklist of all they needed to do in Royal. Beyond ensuring Blackwood Bank and its customers were now well protected, she still had details to oversee with the Royal Gives Back gala that Buckley had requested, and she wanted to be available for Lulu as the wedding date neared.

"The new data protection software is in place for the bank." He spoke with reassuring confidence. "We can send out a joint press release about that as soon as you or Vaughn approve the copy my PR department submitted for your review."

Mulling over the idea, she had to admit it sounded good to set her mind at ease about work. But she voiced the concern that held her back.

"Assuming we do this—and I appreciate the generous offer—what does it mean for us? It bears dis-

cussion as we start spending more time together."
She wasn't sure about his expectations and she didn't
want to confuse the issue. "That is, we haven't spoken about where this relationship might lead. You
know I'm not staying in Royal."

Reaching across the table, he laid his hand over
hers. The touch was tender, yet it stirred butterflies
and memories, a wealth of feeling in that simple connection.

"What if we simply enjoy the time we have instead of worrying about what will happen at the end
of the month?" His words cast a spell separate from
his touch, tapping into the secret wishes of her heart
and old, dangerous longings. "You've got a lot on
your plate right now without adding me to the list
of things you have to resolve."

It felt reckless to run headlong, heedless of consequences, into something that could cause her a world
of hurt. And yet she found herself wanting to agree,
just so their affair didn't have to end. She didn't know
what she wanted long term, but the thought of ending
things with Kai right now caused a pain that was almost physical. Could she trust him not to pull away
from her the way he had the last time? Or would she
be the one to pull away when she finished her duties
in Texas and returned to New York? They had only
a few more weeks before Royal Gives Back.

Surely she could keep her heart safe for just a
little longer.

"In that case," she began, threading her fingers

through his where their hands rested on the table, "I'd love to fly to New York with you."

"You went *where*?" Kai's brother's voice was curt over the phone. Dane sounded more than a little agitated.

Kai juggled the cell while he continued to work on his tablet in a chauffeured Range Rover. He sat in midtown traffic at rush hour, having dropped off Miranda at the Goddess headquarters. He was doing his damnedest to stay out of her way and let her use the time in Manhattan to conduct her business, but the moment she exited the private SUV, he'd begun making plans for their evening together.

His window of opportunity with her was narrowing as the end of the month approached, and he planned to pull out all the stops to romance her. That meant dinner and dancing at one of the most beautiful and exclusive rooftop bars in the city. He'd asked an assistant to review Miranda's episodes of *Secret Lives of NYC Ex-Wives* to learn any intelligence about her favorite places, and the Chelsea restaurant was a spot she'd exclaimed over in the first season. Kai had spent a small fortune to have the place to themselves on short notice. But before he could finish making preparations for the evening, he needed to deal with his brother.

"I flew to New York with Miranda," Kai explained. "Madtec has two clients I can see while I'm here."

"What about Blackwood Bank?" Dane swore on the other end of the call, and from the rhythmic thumping in the background, Kai guessed his brother was taking out his aggravation by running the green stairwell they'd installed in their building to use like a gym. "Reporters have been breathing down our necks all day."

"The situation is well in hand or I wouldn't have left the office yesterday." Kai leaned back in the leather seat, glancing out the window to see if they'd made progress. He had a meeting downtown in ten minutes. "The joint press release went out, so if the newshounds want a story, just keep referring back to the talking points. The data breach is old news."

"Is it, though?" The thumping on Dane's end of the call slowed and then stopped. He was breathing hard now. "I don't like the resentful tone I'm picking up in the tech community about the way we rolled out the new software during a PR crisis."

Kai frowned, his nerves drawing tight with foreboding. "What do you mean?"

"Face it, Kai. The bank data breach might have catapulted our cybersecurity software into national recognition if it ends up working as well as we think it's going to." Dane huffed out a long breath and then lowered his voice. "There are bound to be detractors who'll suggest we pulled some kind of unethical stunt to put ourselves in the position to be the white knights—and gain lots of publicity—given our... er, *my* history."

Kai knew Dane was referring to his stint in jail—
to their shared hacking history that had been well
publicized. Yet he still couldn't believe what he was
hearing. He double-checked the partition window
between him and SUV's driver, stabbing it hard with
his finger to ensure it was sealed tightly.

"Are you suggesting that people are saying we organized a major breach of one of our own clients in
order to draw media attention to our bringing a new
protection software product to market?" The repercussions of that kind of publicity nightmare could
be devastating for a fledgling business. Madtec was
only just beginning to realize full legitimacy in the
tech marketplace. This could ruin their credibility
with any business that might be thinking of hiring
them.

For that matter, what would Miranda think of the
rumors? She'd never been comfortable with the idea
that many successful tech gurus had skirted the law
to learn the business, testing the bounds of cybersecurity by quietly hacking it. Her opinion mattered to
him, and not just because of their business affiliation.

"I'm saying it's an excellent possibility." Dane
sounded weary and more than a little ticked off. "It's
already being speculated about among the tech elite.
It's probably only a matter of time before a story like
that finds traction with a wider audience."

"We need to track those rumors and put a stop to
them." Kai opened a new screen on his tablet and
got to work, firing off a message to the overworked

press relations advocate at Madtec. "I'll be back in Deer Springs tomorrow, but I'll see what I can find out from here to squash the story."

Disconnecting the call, Kai realized the SUV was slowing outside his appointment with the city's major public transportation provider. He'd been working with them for months to increase their cybersecurity and had been glad to wrangle a last-minute meeting today. But it would take a superhuman effort to redirect his thoughts to this project right now when the fear of negative repercussions from the Blackwood Bank scandal threatened Madtec.

And his relationship with Miranda.

More than anything, he simply wanted to focus on making tonight a memorable experience for her. Because somehow, she'd slid straight past his defenses for the second time in his life, and he refused to waste this opportunity to woo her and win.

Stepping inside the custom closet in her Brooklyn brownstone that evening, Miranda took pleasure in the sight of her full wardrobe for the first time in months. Being able to dress for her date tonight with Kai would be all the more enjoyable for having access to her things. Because yes, she wanted to knock his socks off. To feel feminine and desirable after the failure of her marriage and the loneliness of the years that followed.

Peering over the rows of shoes carefully stored in protective clear bins, Miranda couldn't shake the unsettling truth that her New York home felt strange to her after spending so much time in Royal. Lonelier, somehow, since she'd formed tentative bonds with Buckley's children.

Not to mention the much more exciting connection she shared with Kai.

Inspired by a pair of sunshine-yellow high-heeled sandals, Miranda turned toward the rack where she kept her gowns to thumb through them for a draped silk gown in a creamy color, printed with greenery and yellow flowers. Kai had texted that he was sending a car for her at seven and would meet her for dinner at a surprise location. He'd indicated the dress was formal for a special evening out, a caveat that only added to her enjoyment in getting ready.

In the days when they'd been a couple in Deer Springs, their dates had been diner visits where they'd sneak a few moments together on her breaks, or rides on his motorcycle. They'd always had fun together without spending money neither of them had, but she looked forward to seeing Kai in a tuxedo and standing next to him in the kind of couture gown she'd once only dreamed of owning. It had taken her a lot of years to give herself this Cinderella moment, but she couldn't deny she took pride in herself for the hard work that made it possible to slide into handmade Italian leather shoes and fasten a bracelet of tiny yellow diamonds around one wrist.

When the sleek black Cadillac arrived for her half

an hour later, the driver greeted her warmly but only smiled when she asked for a hint about her destination, ratcheting up the suspense, anticipation…desire.

What did Kai have in mind?

She was glad to think about the night ahead instead of her earlier meeting with her competitor, AMuse. The offer they'd made for a joint venture to go global had been exciting, but it also added a new complication to her already uncertain future. There'd been a time when she wouldn't have had to think twice about an offer like that. The opportunity to take the Goddess brand to other countries was exciting. A natural extension of her business plan. Yet it would make seeing Kai all but impossible down the road. Bad enough she was based in New York and he was based in Texas. But if she began traveling internationally to make the new venture with AMuse happen, she wouldn't ever have time to work on a relationship.

Not that Kai had hinted he wanted to continue seeing her once she left Royal. For tonight, she simply wanted to enjoy whatever Kai had planned.

The driver slowed down in front of a brick building in Chelsea, and it took Miranda a moment to recognize the plain black awning and black double doors with a discreet pineapple insignia beside them. Anticipation swelled when she recognized the facade to her favorite rooftop venue in Manhattan. How had Kai guessed?

A warm spring breeze teased her bare shoulders as she emerged from the vehicle, and a doorman appeared to escort her inside. This time, she didn't try to pry hints from him. She merely stepped into the elevator he indicated, surprised that the building seemed quiet at this hour. The lower floors were home to a unique, immersive theater experience and the restaurant and bar on the upper levels were usually packed, especially when the weather was this ideal.

Reaching the top level, the elevator doors slid open to reveal the rooftop bar swathed in green just the way she remembered. Lightweight vines climbed high structural arches. White lights wound through the greens and stretched overhead to put a network of tiny stars almost in reach. Live violin music—more formal than the sounds of the usual bar scene—played softly from a duo in a far corner.

But, strangely, the bar was otherwise empty until a devastatingly handsome man stepped out from behind a row of potted flowering trees. His face was illuminated by the white lights overhead and the hurricane lamps that crowded a nearby table.

Kai.

Her heartbeat quickened at the sight of him. Clean-shaven and dressed in a tuxedo custom fit to his athletic frame, he looked like a man born to the finer things in life. Desire for him, and all the delectable ways he could make her feel, curled warmly in her belly.

"You look incredible, Miranda." He walked forward to greet her with a debonair kiss that lingered on the back of her fingers. He held her gaze as his mouth grazed her skin.

The feel of his lips on her skin stirred fresh longing. Tingly sensations zipped up her spine and back down again.

"Thank you." She noticed he didn't let go of her hand, keeping her fingers wrapped in his. Her gaze wandered over the lines of his black silk jacket where it skimmed his broad shoulders and tapered to his narrow waist and hips. "The tux suits you, Kai. I wasn't expecting such a special night when you offered a spur-of-the-moment trip."

"I thought it was time to make my intentions toward you known," he countered, leading her farther from the musicians to a spot near the edge of the rooftop terrace.

They had a clear view of the lighted spires from skyscrapers in lower Manhattan when he took her in his arms for a slow dance. Her body followed his easily, one hand landing on his shoulder while he kept hold of the other.

"What intentions might those be?" Her pulse hammered harder, uncertain what she wanted or hoped to hear.

She thought she knew better than to get involved with Kai again, and yet here they were, unable to stay away from each other.

"I want to remind you how good it can be between

us, Miranda." His forehead tipped toward hers. "Last time we were together, I let outside influences come between us."

A chill feathered through her as she remembered the way her mother had interfered, planting the seeds of doubt in Kai's mind about their future together.

As much as she wanted to make the most of their evening and push aside outside concerns, she found her current doubts harder to ignore. The offer from AMuse circled around her brain.

"What happens when I leave Royal at the end of the month?" she asked, peering deep into his green eyes, desperate for answers that had proved all too elusive to her. "I have a whole life in New York. And today, my competitor suggested a joint venture that would take Goddess global."

Kai's smile was as unexpected as it was unmistakable. "That's fantastic, Miranda." He squeezed her gently. "Congratulations. You deserve this."

"Thank you." A surge of pride swelled. After all the times she and Kai had sat in the Deer Springs Diner together, figuring out how to make their dreams come true, it felt like she'd come full circle to savor this business victory with him here, dancing on a rooftop under the twinkle of white lights and the glow of the city's skyline. "I've been so focused on how it would work that I haven't taken a moment to really celebrate the achievement."

"That changes now," he insisted. "I hope you'll let

me celebrate with you over dinner. We'll see what the server can find for a fitting champagne to toast the moment."

The lilting tune they'd been dancing to shifted, slowing down a bit. Kai's steps matched the cadence, easily guiding her while she tried to put her finger on what was bothering her about celebrating the news with him.

"I appreciate that. And I'd love some champagne. But I wonder how hard this would make things for work and—" she hesitated as her hair blew softly against her cheek "—for me, personally. It would mean a lot more travel."

She didn't spell out her concerns about seeing him after she left Texas, mainly because she wasn't sure if he saw her departure as an obvious end date for their affair.

"There was a time when we wouldn't have let logistics dictate our future." He seemed unconcerned. But did that mean he wasn't counting on a long-distance relationship in the first place?

She didn't ask because she didn't know what she wanted either.

"And yet we both have too much at stake to walk away from businesses we've worked hard to create." The fact that they were even discussing it worried her a little. But it excited her too, stirring a forgotten hopefulness.

Could they find a way to make it work?

The distant sounds of New York nightlife drifting up from the street provided a soft background to the violins' romantic melody.

"For tonight, it's enough if I can just prove to you that we were meant to be together." He twirled her under his arm as the music stopped altogether. When it ended, he pulled her against him for a long, slow, thorough taste.

She sank into him, wanting to burn the memory of this moment into her brain to preserve it forever. To look back on when she left Texas for good and resumed her life in New York without him. With the end of their affair in sight, she was eager to keep the outside world at bay, the moment sweetly dream-like with the soft breeze blowing her silk gown against her legs, and Kai's strong arms holding her close. His lips were soft and teasing at first, then lingered until she felt breathless.

When he eased away, she opened her eyes slowly.

"Is that why you went to all the trouble of booking this amazing venue just for us?" she asked, curious about what this over-the-top evening truly meant. "To show me how well you know what I like?"

"To show you there's nothing I wouldn't do for you, Miranda." His green eyes were serious, and her heart turned over in her chest.

Romantic words. They fluttered around her with teasing promise like the spring breeze. But could she trust them?

"For tonight, I just want to be with you," she admitted, not ready to think beyond the here and now.

Because after her failed marriage, she couldn't afford to be wrong about love again.

Ten

With the temptation of Miranda Dupree seated beside him, Kai willed the driver to go faster as their private car sped over Manhattan Bridge later that night, leaving the New York skyline behind them. He'd enjoyed every moment spent with Miranda tonight, but the need to be really, truly alone with her burned hotter than ever.

"Thank you for celebrating with me tonight." Miranda turned her liquid-blue eyes on him as her fingers covered his on the expanse of leather seat between them. "Sometimes I get so caught up in achieving the next goal I forget to enjoy the milestones as they come. This was…nice. Better than nice, actually. It was an unforgettable night."

Her happiness made all the effort he'd put into the evening well worth it. He took his time threading his fingers through hers, relishing the simple connection even as he craved a far more intimate one. With his other hand, he stabbed the button to raise the privacy window to prevent the driver from overhearing them. Or seeing them.

"The celebrating isn't over, as far as I'm concerned." He lifted her palm to his mouth and pressed a kiss in the center. "I hope to make the night more memorable for you soon."

He heard her swift intake of breath as he kissed his way past her wrist. Over the delicate skin of her inner arm. The scent of her fragrant skin—soap and jasmine—teased his nose as she shifted closer, her knee brushing his.

Electricity crackled between them. He lifted his attention from her arm to the soft swell of her breasts over the low neckline of her cream-colored dress. Her chest rose and fell quickly. Her lips parted in silent invitation.

An invitation he couldn't afford to indulge until they were alone. Because once he started kissing her, he wouldn't stop. He settled for cupping her chin and running his thumb over the full softness of her mouth.

"How much longer until we reach your place?" he wondered aloud, thinking he could put the time to more satisfying use for them both.

She turned to peer over her shoulder and look out the window as they drove deeper into Brooklyn.

"My street is next," she replied, straightening in her seat. "We're in luck."

A damned good thing given the way the sparks between them flared hotter with each passing second. A few moments later, the vehicle slowed on a tree-lined street in front of a row of brownstones. After helping Miranda from the vehicle and exchanging a few words with the driver about the next day's itinerary, Kai forced himself to take an extra moment to admire her quiet neighborhood before following her up the steps to the tall, black double doors that served as the main entrance. No sense crowding or rushing her. She had to know how much he wanted her. She'd already disarmed the alarm on the keypad by the door.

He stood in the foyer while she locked and reset the alarm. The long, narrow foyer was dimly lit from the hall sconces, but Kai could see the whitewashed brick fireplace and pocket doors that gave the home a historic feel. The low, modern furnishings and industrial chandelier were obvious touches of the current owner, however.

Before he could compliment her on the house, Miranda was in his arms, reminding him exactly why they'd been in such a hurry to get here. Her arms locked around his neck, breasts pressed to his chest in a way that made him forget everything else. She kissed along his jaw while he molded her to him, his hands tracing her curves through the silky fabric of her printed gown.

"Where's your room?" he asked, his breath coming fast.

She unfastened two buttons of his shirt before pointing toward the staircase. "Second floor."

They ascended the steps together, her hand wrapped in his, legs brushing on the way up.

She led him to the left where the master suite awaited. Inside the open archway, her bed stood in front of another fireplace. Here, everything was white and gray. A color scheme that would normally be calming if he wasn't on fire to have her. A single orchid bloomed by the bed. The blinds over the bay windows were already lowered so that the room was lit only by the white glow spilling from the open door of the en suite bath.

A beautiful space for an even more beautiful woman. She had so damned much to be proud of. She was vibrant. Independent. Fearless. And Kai wanted her more than he'd ever thought possible to want any woman.

Not ready to vocalize that until he figured out what it meant for them, he tucked a finger underneath his bow tie and freed the knot before unfastening the top button of his shirt. Miranda's gaze heated. A small smile curved one side of her lips.

She answered him by slipping off the straps of her gown. First one. Then the other.

Damn, but he was crazy about her.

When he shrugged out of his shirt, she stepped out of her shoes, her toes disappearing in the thick white carpet beneath their feet.

"Turn around." He reached for her hips to bring her closer. "I'll unzip you."

She pivoted to present him with her back. He lowered the zipper slowly, stroking touches along each new square inch of silky skin he bared.

When the gown sagged and fell to her feet, he anchored her to him with an arm around her waist. Skimming her hair away from her jasmine-scented neck, he kissed a trail from beneath her ear to her shoulder and back again. Unhooking her pale green bra, he let that slip to the floor too, his attention fixed on the taut peaks of her breasts. She shimmied against him, her hips rocking back into his as a low moan vibrated through her.

The last shreds of his restraint disintegrated.

Miranda was on fire.

Spinning in Kai's arms, she couldn't undress him fast enough, desire fogging her brain and making her fingers fumble awkwardly with the fastening of his tuxedo pants. She needed him naked with an urgency she'd only ever experienced with him.

He peeled off her panties while she dragged down his boxers, their arms bumping and hooking. Not that it mattered. Nothing mattered but being with him.

He lifted her to deposit her in the middle of her bed, a smooth drop into the soft, thick comforter.

She had a moment to savor the way he looked when he retrieved a condom from a pocket of the discarded clothing. His square shoulders were backlit by the light from the bathroom, the outline of him deliciously masculine. Unquestionably powerful. When he stepped closer, the rippled muscles of his abs caught her eye, but only for a moment before her gaze shifted to his hips and the rigid length of him that awaited her touch.

Yet when she reached for him, he pinned both her hands lightly, his gaze probing hers as he covered her.

"I need you too much to wait another minute." His ragged words made hot pleasure curl in her belly. "I've wanted you all night."

Anticipation and excitement twined together, rendering her breathless. Light-headed.

"No more than I've wanted you." She liked knowing what she did to him, relieved that she wasn't alone in this out-of-control hunger.

With his gaze locked on hers, he let go of her wrists to curve a hand around her hip, tilting her toward him. She bit her lip against the exquisite feel of him sliding inside her. Deeper.

When she realized her fingernails were digging into his shoulder, she let go, kissing the place where she'd left red crescent moons. Wrapping her arms around his neck, she held on to him, letting him set the pace while the rhythm of it carried her away.

Each stroke was pleasure filled. Each breath brought her closer to a climax she wasn't ready for. Not yet.

She wanted this night to last and last. Not just because of how it felt to have him with her. In her.

But because she couldn't imagine letting go of Kai again.

The realization slid into her consciousness at the same time he whispered her name in her ear, the sound of it and the feel of his breath making her shiver. Sending her hurtling toward the release she couldn't possibly stave off another moment.

She clung to him, her body undulating with waves of sweet sensations she never wanted to end. In the midst of it, she registered that she'd taken him with her, her body teasing him to his own completion.

They held each other for long moments afterward, breathing raggedly, heartbeats pounding madly. When, finally, those slowed down, Kai settled on her right side. The overhead ceiling fan stirred cool air over them, but he tucked her closer. She felt around for the edge of the duvet and draped it over them both.

He sifted his fingers through her hair, relaxing her enough to chase latent worries about their future from her brain. She was almost asleep in his arms when he whispered to her.

"I hope you're going to take the deal with AMuse." He spoke softly, but her eyes fluttered open to fix on his in the dim light. "It's the culmination of everything you've worked so hard for."

It definitely wasn't pillow talk, or sweet nothings whispered in her ear. She held her breath for a moment, wondering what it meant for him. Why he'd shared that thought with her now. Was it his way of setting her free after her time in Royal was done? Or was it a genuine encouragement for her to embrace the dreams she'd always had for her business? Seeing nothing but warmth and thoughtfulness in his eyes, she forced herself to let out her breath.

"I know," she admitted, tracing circles on his chest. She felt grateful at least that he understood her even if he wouldn't always be a part of her life. But thinking about a future without him in it hurt. "I probably will."

His nod was a fraction of movement. His eyes closed then, as if he felt his role in the decision was finished. He'd encouraged her to do what she wanted.

For the first time, she acknowledged that Kai was more than just a passionate lover. She'd been wrong to write off what they'd shared in the past as simple chemistry that wouldn't stand up to the tests of time. He was her friend. And he wanted what was best for her.

But was that enough to keep them together through a long-distance separation? Her chest ached at the idea of leaving, but she also couldn't possibly stay. So for now, she closed her eyes and told herself to keep breathing. One way or another, she'd have to figure it out.

* * *

Kai awoke to his cell phone vibrating.

He'd been so deeply asleep beside Miranda that it took him a moment to orient himself and realize that he was still in her Brooklyn brownstone after their impromptu trip to New York City. Sliding from the covers, Kai reached for his phone and answered it, even as he tucked the duvet tighter around Miranda. He regretted leaving her side one of the few times he'd been able to sleep beside her.

He gathered up a fistful of clothes from the floor before he made his way into the adjoining bathroom so he wouldn't wake her. There, he closed the door silently before speaking.

"What's up?" he asked quietly, meeting his own gaze in the huge mirror over the marble vanity. He knew it had to be his brother since Dane's number was the only one allowed to ring through at this hour.

Well, Dane's and Miranda's. But obviously *she* hadn't phoned him.

"Disaster is what's up." Dane spewed the words like hot lava, voice raised and angry. "The rumors about Madtec orchestrating the Blackwood Bank breach have gone national. A major news organization picked up the story."

Dread enveloped Kai's gut. Juggling the phone, he stepped into his boxers.

"Rumors aren't news," he answered reflexively, hoping like hell his brother was overreacting.

"Seriously? Have you read what gets shared for

news nowadays, man?" Dane spoke fast, each word punching through the phone. "It doesn't matter if it's true. The suspicions raised will cripple the business—"

"Hold up." Kai stepped into his pants, noting that the sun was rising, a low light filtering in through the stained glass window. He needed to get on top of this. Fast. "Send me a link where I can get up to speed, and I'll call you back."

His brother swore, but pinged him an address to read the story.

Disconnecting the call, Kai sank to the white tile tub surround and scrolled through the article along with the comments before checking a couple of social media platforms. Dane hadn't overstated the case. Madtec needed a full-scale response to the bad press if they wanted any chance of overcoming this.

He texted his brother and his head of public relations to set up a virtual meeting in an hour. First, he needed to wake Miranda. He needed to be back in Deer Springs. Regret that their night together had to end this way stung hard. But she would understand.

Tossing his phone aside, he sat on the mattress near Miranda and touched her shoulder through the covers. Her eyelids fluttered, and he wondered what it would be like to wake up beside this woman day after day. He was falling for her.

Hard.

The realization threaded through the tension of the day, tightening it all into a hard knot. He couldn't afford to think about long term with her yet. Not when she was going to be building her brand overseas and working out of Manhattan while he was in Deer Springs.

"Miranda?" He watched as she came upright in bed slowly, dragging the covers with her.

"What is it? Is everything okay?" Her blue eyes darted around him, taking in his clothes before shifting to the clock on the wall.

More than anything, he wanted to slide back into bed beside her. To relive their incredible night together. But that was no longer possible.

He flipped on the bedside lamp.

"I need to fly home. Madtec is under assault in the press because of rumors that we someone how orchestrated the Blackwood Bank breach." Sharing the words made it hit hard all over again. Just when he'd finally thought Madtec had gained the legitimacy and credibility they needed.

Fighting to prove himself over and over again was getting old.

"I don't understand." Miranda shook her head, a crumbled red curl wavering as she moved. "Why would anyone suggest your company would launch a cyberattack on the business you were hired to protect? It makes no sense."

Frustration flared. "I wouldn't think so either. But it's been suggested that we fabricated the security breach in order to show off our new software. Our detractors have gained traction with the idea that our saving a giant like Blackwood Bank was perfect—and free—advertising for the new encryption software."

Miranda's blue gaze faltered, a shadow passing through their depths. But then she seemed to hide her reaction, her lips pursing in thought before she spoke again. "That's ludicrous."

A moment passed as he tried to process what he'd seen. But it damned well looked like she doubted him.

"You can't think I'd do something like that... Do you?" he asked, feeling like the ground had been yanked out from under him.

He'd worked his ass off to prove himself in the business world. But it had never occurred to him that Miranda would question his ethics.

"Of course not," she assured him, as if he hadn't seen her doubt with his own eyes. Perhaps being so newly awake made it tougher to hide her real feelings.

She glanced down at the duvet where she picked at the white binding on the cotton cover. "It's just—for a moment—I was remembering what you told me about the tech community. That most of the giants who understand the industry best are the people who started like you and Dane—hacking."

The sense of betrayal shook him. He stiffened his spine against it.

"So you figured it was only natural we'd undermine our own clients for the sake of some good press." He understood now why total strangers could think it of him and Dane, when the woman he cared about so much could come to the same sickening conclusion about him.

"No." She sounded more certain now, but it didn't erase the flash of doubt. "I came to Madtec because you're the best, Kai. End of story."

Woodenly, he stood. He refused to think about how close he'd come to losing his heart to this woman all over again. Only to be stomped twice as hard as the first time.

"Either way, I need to return to Deer Springs." His problems had only multiplied by sharing them with Miranda. Funny, now the potential loss of his business reputation didn't feel nearly as daunting as the loss of her. "The pilot can be at the airfield in an hour, so I'll call a car as soon as you're ready."

For a moment, he thought she'd argue. Or somehow try to retract the way she'd just leveled him with her lack of faith in him.

But then, she simply nodded.

Kai turned on his heel and left her to get ready on her own. The sooner he got back to Texas, the better.

He belonged there. As for Miranda Dupree and her global success? She'd have to pursue her dreams without him, the same way she always had.

Eleven

A week after the disastrous conclusion to the New York City trip, Miranda stood on the front steps of the Pine Valley estate that Sophie Blackwood Townshend now shared with Nigel. Miranda clutched a bouquet in one hand and a basket of cookies and pastries from a local bakery in the other. She was overdue to congratulate Sophie on her pregnancy news in person, but it had been a long, heart-wrenching week since her misstep with Kai.

He'd barely spoken to her on their flight back to Royal. Of course, she'd understood he was in the middle of a business crisis with Madtec's reputation under attack. But she suspected that he'd been more upset by her moment of doubt than any of the rumors, and that had given her plenty of pangs of conscience since then.

It wasn't that she believed he was unethical. It was just… Well, she'd been waiting for the other shoe to drop from the moment they'd reignited their affair.

She shoved those thoughts to the side, however, as a young liveried housekeeper with a long blond ponytail opened the door of Sophie's pretty French country estate.

"Hello." Miranda smiled at the woman. "I'm here to see Sophie—"

"Thank God for a visitor," Sophie's unmistakable voice rang out from the back of the house. "Tell her I'm in the kitchen, Josephine!"

The petite housekeeper grinned at the same time Miranda did.

"I'll find her." Miranda nodded her thanks while the housekeeper shut the door. "Thank you."

"Miranda, is that you?" Sophie asked, peering out of the kitchen, a glass of water in her hand. At twenty-seven years old, Sophie had long auburn hair and brown eyes. She had killer curves and a quick wit, always ready with a smile. As the baby of the Blackwood clan and the only daughter, she'd been beloved by all. "I'm so glad you're here. Nigel practically keeps me housebound on a steady diet of constant calories, so I don't faint again." Her gaze went to the basket. "Although I'll bet whatever is in that basket is the kind of calories I'll actually enjoy."

Warmth suffused Miranda's heart to be welcomed

this way by the stepdaughter she'd once feared would hate her forever. Sophie had still been a teenager when Miranda married Buckley, and Sophie had strongly resented their relationship. After the reading of the will, Sophie had put all her considerable efforts into proving Miranda was up to no good by infiltrating Green Room Media in New York to dig up dirt on her ex-stepmother. Dirt she hoped to use to get the will overturned in court.

The fact that they were finally able to put those years of ill will behind them was nothing short of a miracle in Miranda's book. She would always be grateful to Buckley for giving her this second chance to be a family with the Blackwoods.

"I got your favorites," Miranda announced, remembering her own efforts to get to know Sophie as a young woman, attempting to buy her favor with treats. She set the basket down on the island of the gleaming white kitchen where Sophie seemed to be preparing a pot of tea at the coffee bar. "And some flowers to congratulate you on your amazing news." Miranda hugged her tightly.

"Thank you." Sophie sniffed the bouquet of hydrangeas and roses. "The flowers are gorgeous. Can I make you some tea?"

"Sure. But why don't you let me do it? You haven't been home from the hospital for very long."

Sophie turned a dark scowl her way before peering into the basket of pastries. "Don't you gang up on me too, Miranda. I'm pregnant, not ill." She withdrew an almond croissant. "Oh, this smells amazing."

While Sophie loaded a plate with some of the pastries, Miranda quietly found spoons and napkins, eager to get the two of them everything they needed so Sophie could sit and rest. Because no matter what Nigel's new wife said, Miranda had just visited the two of them in the hospital, so clearly Sophie needed to be mindful of her health.

Of course, thinking of that visit made Miranda remember how thoughtful and kind Kai had been to personally drive her to Royal that night. She'd missed him to the point of pain this past week, but she reminded herself to focus on Sophie as she carried the mugs and spoons to the breakfast bar in the huge, open kitchen.

"So what did the doctor have to say, Sophie?" she pressed, gesturing for the younger woman to take a seat on one of the padded leather stools. "Why did you faint at the airport?"

"Probably because we were going through customs in a crowded airport with a crush of other people and I hadn't eaten since the night before. I slept the whole flight." Sophie slid onto one of the stools while Miranda carried over the teapot and pastries. "If I'd known I was pregnant I would have packed a protein bar or something. But as it was…*whoosh*. Down I went. I scared Nigel half to death."

"I'm sure you did," Miranda mused as she took the stool beside Sophie, enjoying the vision of those two very different personalities spending their lives together. Sophie was so bubbly and warm, while Nigel was reserved to the point that he could be mistaken for aloof—unless, of course, you happened to see him when he was looking at Sophie.

Clinking the pot against Miranda's mug, Sophie lifted it to pour, the pointed sleeves of a colorful caftan trailing over her hand.

"But now he's completely overcompensating, expecting me to eat constantly and stay close to home." She rolled her eyes. "Although the honeymoon was so amazing, I guess I can forgive him."

A sly, happy smile curved her lips.

"I'm so glad for you both." Miranda felt another pang of envy for all the love and happiness around her while she floundered around trying to get her own life in order. She'd just finished celebrating one wedding and now Lulu's was the week after the Royal Gives Back gala. "I hope you'll both be at the Royal Gives Back event?"

"We wouldn't miss it." After pouring her own tea, Sophie slid into the leather counter stool beside Miranda. "I think of it as Dad's 'coming out' party, where the rest of the world will finally know his good qualities."

They drank their tea in silence for a moment, perhaps equally wrapped up in their own memories of Buckley Blackwood. He'd been a blowhard and a tough businessman, always hiding his softer side while he'd been alive, even with his family. And while Miranda was happy he was finally going to be celebrated for the good person he was underneath the unyielding facade, she knew it would have made a lot of people in his life happier if he could have been more giving—and forgiving—while he'd still been alive.

She didn't want to be the kind of person who made the same mistakes over and over again her whole life. And yet hadn't she ended up back in the same place with Kai as she'd been ten years ago? The new rift between them hurt even more than the first time.

Sophie broke the silence when she set her cup back on the granite countertop, the scent of chamomile and lemon rising from the tea. "I heard from Vaughn this morning that things are running smoothly at the bank again after the security breach."

Miranda's breath caught, her thoughts flying straight back to Kai, the man who'd steered the bank through the chaos.

"We were fortunate to have Madtec helping us through that nightmare," Miranda said, missing Kai even more. She nibbled on a raspberry tart, wondering how she'd ever get over him.

Would he even speak to her again? Or had he checked out on her for good this time? She'd hoped he'd be at the Royal Gives Back gala, but maybe he wouldn't bother attending now.

"No doubt." Sophie slanted a sideways gaze in her direction. "How about you, Miranda? Did *you* feel fortunate to have Kai Maddox back in your life after so many years?"

Miranda didn't miss the arch note in Sophie's voice.

She spun to look at her.

"You knew I dated Kai?" she asked. Had Sophie just learned about this when the tabloids showed her and Kai leaving Madtec's offices together? Or had she known before? But no, surely if she'd known years ago, it would have come up when Miranda had first married Buckley.

Back then, Sophie had been so eager to do anything that might get under Miranda's skin.

"Of course. You forget how eager I was to see you trip up as Dad's new wife when he brought you to Blackwood Hollow." She didn't sound proud of the fact anymore. She stirred more sugar into her tea, the spoon clinking softly against the sides of the mug before she withdrew it and laid it on a napkin. "I made it my mission to learn whatever I could about your past. I hoped to catch you cheating, but nothing ever happened. You stayed loyal, even when things weren't working out in your marriage. Even I couldn't find fault with how you treated Dad, as hard as I tried. You were good to him, Miranda."

She released a pent-up breath, grateful she felt that way. "I tried to be. But I failed as a wife to Buckley. And it looks like I failed with Kai again."

Sophie swiveled in her seat to look at her head-on. "What do you mean?"

"I mean we were seeing each other again. Up until last week." Miranda hadn't told anyone about what happened with Kai. Not even the other *Ex-Wives*. But she felt the need to share it with someone, and Sophie had always been candid with her—even in the years when she hadn't been kind. Maybe she needed that candidness right now. "I was rattled when he told me about the scandal surrounding Madtec and the rumors that he and his brother had somehow engineered the breach for the publicity."

"You believed that?" Sophie's auburn eyebrow arched.

Clutching the warmth of her mug with both hands, Miranda felt like even more of a heel.

"Not really. But for a moment, I suppose, it sounded like something he might have done back in the days when he walked the knife's edge between right and wrong." He'd been so desperate to learn back then, even if it meant crossing some lines. But he wasn't that desperate kid anymore. She knew how much the reputation of his business meant to him. Not to mention the reputation of his brother, who'd gone to jail for something Kai felt like he should have prevented.

"So tell him you were wrong." Sophie underscored the advice by pointing at her with a fig cookie. "No one knows better than me that sometimes a big, fat apology is in order. I've had to give a lot of them since I've jumped to my fair share of wrong conclusions. But if you're sincere—"

"There are so many more things that aren't right between us though, Sophie. My life is in New York and his is here. I have the show, and an offer to take Goddess global—"

She halted herself abruptly as Sophie was shaking her head, her long auburn hair swinging. "That's all a smokescreen. And none of it really matters if you love each other. First you apologize. Then you can see if any of the rest of it has any bearing on your relationship. My two cents says that it won't."

Miranda wasn't so sure. But she understood what Sophie was saying.

Reaching for her, she squeezed Sophie's forearm. "When did you turn so wise?"

"A miracle, right?" Sophie laughed. "I guess I had to make my own share of missteps before I figured out how to be a better person. I hurt you, and I hurt Nigel with my headstrong ways, so convinced I knew it all. But part of being a strong person means learning to back down when you're wrong."

Miranda felt the unfamiliar prick of warmth in her eyes and she swallowed back a lump in her throat. She wasn't sure if the knot of feelings were for all she'd been through in her role as the Wicked Stepmother to Buckley's kids, or if it was because of how she'd handled things with Kai. But she appreciated Sophie's words.

She needed to decide if she was going to take the plunge and come to terms with everything she felt for Kai. She'd been hiding behind her defenses and her boundaries for too long. Maybe all of it was a smokescreen, after all.

"You're right." Miranda nodded, glad she'd come. "Thank you, Sophie."

"Of course. That's what families are for." Sophie winked at her. "Do you need any help with the gala? I'm really ready for a new project—"

"Nigel would have my head, and we both know it," Miranda reminded her. "I'll just be happy having you both there."

"We're looking forward to it," Sophie assured her.

An hour later, Miranda left Pine Valley and headed back to Royal to finish her preparations for Royal Gives Back. It would be her last task in town on Buckley's behalf, but she planned to stay for a week afterward for Lulu's wedding. The wedding would be the season finale of their show.

After that, there would be no excuse for her to remain in Royal any longer. Unless, of course, she convinced Kai to take a chance on continuing their relationship. Something she couldn't deny that she wanted more than air.

Because she knew now—after this miserable week of hurting without him—that she loved him. Now, more than ever. She hadn't wanted to face it, fearing how much it might hurt, but she'd fallen for him anyhow.

Maybe she'd sabotaged things with him purposely so she wouldn't have to face the hurt of rejection a second time. Whatever her reason, she refused to let Kai think she believed the worst of him.

That wasn't fair to him.

She just needed to find the right time to tell him before the gala. Then, she'd hope for the best. No matter how much it hurt.

Kai ignored the phone messages from Miranda the day before the Royal Gives Back Gala.

Amad had walked into his office with two of them earlier in the week. And now, the day before the gala, there'd been another.

Kai couldn't say why he was avoiding her—out of a need to protect himself from hearing her say goodbye, or to maintain the anger he still felt that she'd believed the worst of him. Thankfully, he'd discovered the source of the smear campaign earlier in the week, and this afternoon he'd had the pleasure of seeing the same tech rival who'd started the rumors now under investigation for breaking the law himself. Alistair Quinn had been a thorn in the Maddox brothers' side for years, but it seemed he wouldn't be making trouble any longer. How ironic that he'd been charged with pulling the kinds of cheap stunts he'd accused Madtec of using.

It was damned satisfying to be vindicated. Madtec had two big job offers roll in just in the last day, their legitimacy cemented for good.

Now, shutting down his workstation for the night, Kai retrieved his jacket and slid his arms in the sleeves. He opened his office door to find Dane and Amad watching replays of a college basketball game on Amad's desktop computer, reviewing the video in slow motion to exclaim over a great basket.

The workday was done, and it was rewarding to see Amad stick around the office to socialize. That kind of atmosphere was what he and Dane had hoped for when they'd created a more employee-centered office space at Madtec. And now, the business was back in good stead with the public. It should have been a day of celebrating, capped off by the sight of his brother smiling and happy.

Except Kai's victory felt hollow without Miranda.

"Hey." Dane straightened as Kai walked into the outer office. "Ready to go out for a drink to celebrate the future of Madtec now that Alistair Quinn is under investigation?"

"I thought I'd take the bike out for a few hours." He hadn't ridden his motorcycle in weeks. Maybe the fresh air would clear out his head.

Ease the red-hot burn in his chest where his personal regrets lived.

Dane frowned. He strode with Kai toward the private elevator that led directly to the parking area. "Let me walk down with you."

Kai nodded, but said nothing. He felt like a countdown clock was ticking in the back of his brain, every second a reminder that Miranda was a moment closer to leaving Texas for good.

As soon as the elevators doors closed silently behind them, Dane turned serious eyes toward him. "What gives?"

"What do you mean? Why would something be wrong just because I want to take the bike out instead of going out for a drink?" Kai pulled his keys from his pants pocket, agitated.

"I mean, the news broke that the company was the target of a deliberately malicious smear campaign by a rival. We're vindicated and we got two big-money offers from huge companies. Our human resources department can't hire people fast enough." Dane ticked off all the good news on his fingers. "Yet you're dragging yourself through the office like you lost your best friend."

Kai stifled the urge to scowl and snarl because he didn't need Dane sniffing around his private life. As the elevator settled on the ground floor, he charged out into the parking area. The late afternoon sun glinted off a windshield, making him blink.

"It's all good news, but I'm fried. I've been working more than not for the past two weeks." He'd poured all of his energy into clearing his name—and Dane's, too.

And to keep himself from thinking about Miranda.

"I'm not buying it." Dane stepped in front of Kai, making him pull up sharply so he didn't run right into him. "Where's Miranda been? You two went to New York together, yet I haven't a heard a word about her or what went down."

The urge to scowl wouldn't be quieted this time. Kai narrowed his gaze.

"Since when do we trade stories about women? You don't see me inserting myself in your private life." He stepped around his brother and continued toward his car, popping open the locks on the coupe from the key fob.

The executive parking area was quiet, deserted. Heat sweltered off the tarmac even though it was almost six o'clock.

"I didn't say anything when you let her go the first time," Dane countered. "But I know you regretted it then, and you're probably going to regret it this time, too."

Kai ground his teeth together, his jaw flexing. "She's the one walking away," he said finally, the words spilling out in spite of him. "She turned her back on what we had then, and she's never believed we could last this time either."

"How convenient you never have to put yourself on the line with her," Dane observed drily, folding his arms over his chest. "I guess if you don't really try, you can't ever fail. Good thinking, Kai."

The sarcasm dripped from his words. Shaking his head, Dane pivoted on his heel to leave.

"I've tried," Kai retorted. But even he had to cringe at the sullen tone in his voice.

Hell.

Dane spun toward him, arms spread wide. "Have you? Because from my point of view, it looks like you've been dodging her since that first day she showed up here with a business opportunity."

He flinched a little at the direct hit.

"True. But I had my reasons." He stalked away from his vehicle, thinking and pacing. "Since then, I've committed to showing her we could be good together."

He'd driven her to the hospital when her family needed her. Flown her to New York. Supported her global expansion.

"I believe you showed her. But that doesn't mean she understood your message as anything other than being helpful." Dane leaned a hip into Kai's car. "Have you *told* her how you feel? Or have you even worked out for yourself whether you love her or not?"

Kai quit pacing, stunned. The words called everything in him to a halt.

Did he love Miranda? Was he *in love* with her?

He'd never acknowledged the idea openly, maybe because he'd been trying his damnedest not to have his heart shredded a second time. But his love for her was so damned much a bedrock of everything he felt that he couldn't believe he'd never brought the feeling up into the sunlight where he could appreciate it. Share it.

Tell her about it.

Hell yes, he loved her.

"I've got to go." He charged toward his car, his feet fueled with purpose.

"Is that a yes?" Dane drummed his fingers on Kai's hood, assessing his brother.

"She's everything to me," Kai told him simply, the truth settling over him with new clarity. "And I've got to make sure she knows it."

He didn't miss Dane's smug smile as he backed up a step while Kai started the car.

Later, he would thank Dane for helping him figure out what to do next. Right now, he needed to get to the Texas Cattleman's Club before the gala kicked off. He wasn't sure of the logistics for how he'd tell Miranda he loved her, and he didn't know if the sentiment would be returned.

But he understood one thing now thanks to Dane. Kai would regret it forever if he didn't at least try to win her back.

Twelve

Just outside the kitchen of the Texas Cattleman's Club, Miranda consulted with the head of catering an hour after the Royal Gives Back gala began. She was grateful to lose herself in the details of the evening to escape the heartbreak of her rift with Kai. She'd been at the venue for two hours before the event kicked off to ensure things ran smoothly, taking a break only to slip into a black crepe cocktail gown with subtly sexy keyhole cutouts at the waist and shoulder.

Once she approved two minor menu changes, Miranda left the caterer to return to the party, walking through an archway draped with white and gold flowers. A few attendees stood in front of the wall of petals taking photos of each other, and Miranda smiled at them as she passed. The musicians were playing a short set of big-band music in the warm-up hour before Miranda took the stage to thank the guests and make a few announcements about Buckley Blackwood's legacy.

She had her notes waiting on the podium, and she had a few surprises to share with the guests. But for now, she took a few moments to peer around the great room that had been outfitted for the night's gala.

Looking for Kai.

She'd counted on seeing him here so she could apologize in person for doubting him. Even though she knew it wouldn't change the pain she'd caused him. Her words would come too late anyhow, since he'd already been cleared of any wrongdoing. She wished she'd driven to Deer Springs earlier in the week—before the news story broke about his tech rival organizing a smear campaign against Madtec. Then, her apology might have meant more. Might have changed things.

Either way, she had to see him tonight once her obligations at the gala were complete. She owed him the words.

Swallowing hard, she tried not to think about him tonight when she had this one final task to manage for Buckley. With an event planner's eye, she went over the room again, noting the huge white and yellow-gold flower arrangements on the tables,

with white roses, daffodils and ranunculus domi-
nating the tall sprays. Black accents kept the theme
quietly elegant, the wrought iron candelabra and
chair backs picking up the more masculine decor
that dominated the remodeled building of the Texas
Cattleman's Club.

Couples milled around the tables and admired
the appetizer stations while cocktail service circu-
lated regularly with specialty drinks of the evening.
Kellan Blackwood and his bride, Irina, circled the
dance floor along with the other couples. Russian-
born Irina had been the quiet beneficiary of Buckley's kindness when he'd given the down-on-her-luck
former mail-order bride a job as his maid to help
her obtain a work visa while she divorced an abu-
sive ex. The woman's green eyes sparkled now as
she clearly enjoyed Kellan's expert moves on the
dance floor, a purple spotlight winking off the bangles on her fringed red dress. She must be nearly
four months pregnant by now, but Miranda would
have never guessed if she hadn't heard the good news
from Kellan two months ago.

While Miranda watched the utterly devoted couple, Kace LeBlanc, Buckley's lawyer and the execu-
tor of his will, drew up to her side. "I'd call this an
unmitigated success," he announced quietly. The attorney was an interesting match for Lulu with his by-
the-book, quiet competence. "You did an outstanding
job with the gala. Buckley would be pleased."

"Thank you." Miranda had been grateful to throw herself into the preparations over the last week when she ached with all she'd lost, missing Kai every moment. And yes, she'd truly wanted to offer up this last tribute to her ex-husband, to give herself much-needed closure to move forward with her life. If only there was a gala she could throw that would somehow fix the way she'd left things with Kai. "I'm thrilled with the turnout, but even more excited about the donations. I think Buckley's kids were all pleased he wanted to support the Stroke Foundation."

Donna-Leigh Westbrook had died too young from a stroke, and her three children—Kellan, Sophie and Vaughn—had reeled from the loss for long afterward. Miranda had witnessed the hurt in their family firsthand.

"And you can double that amount," Kace confided, leaning closer to make the comment for her ears alone. "Nigel Townshend just told me Green Room Media wants to match whatever we raise tonight. You can announce it when you take the podium."

"That's fantastic news." She was pleased and overwhelmed. If only she didn't feel like she was missing a piece of herself tonight with Kai's absence. "Are you set for the wedding next weekend?"

A smile curved Kace's lips, his normally serious expression transforming. "Honestly? I can't wait."

As if on cue, Lulu hurried over to them, her hands

already outstretched to take Kace's, her diamond engagement ring flashing under the lights.

"Hello, gorgeous Miranda," she drawled, even though she never glanced Miranda's way. She twirled in front of Kace, her sapphire-blue gown fanning around her ankles at the kick-pleat. "I must borrow my man for a dance."

"Lulu—" Kace sounded like he wanted to protest, but he stretched his hands out to hers and let Lulu tug him toward the dance floor.

Faced with all these happy couples, loneliness hovered over Miranda like dark clouds, even in the midst of all the partygoers. Actually, maybe being among these happy, smiling people only increased her own sense of loss. She'd hoped to see Kai here, but now that it seemed like he wasn't going to show, she suspected she could slip away unnoticed from the party after her announcements were made.

She would drive to Deer Springs and speak to him in person. She had an apology to make and some news to deliver about a decision she'd made about her future.

Course set, she spun away from the dance floor and headed toward the podium. She was about to give the bandleader a nod to end the set when Kellan Blackwood intercepted her. Dressed in a tuxedo, Buckley's oldest son had dark brown hair that he'd always worn short, with blue eyes that crinkled at the corners. He looked happy tonight.

"Great party, Miranda." He folded her in a quick hug that reminded her how far she'd come with the Blackwood heirs in the last few months. There'd been a time they'd been certain she was a gold digger. "I'm bringing Irina something to eat, but I wanted to let you know we found out that she's having a boy."

Touched that he'd sought her out to share the news with her, Miranda smiled, genuinely happy for them. They deserved every bit of happiness they'd found together and she refused to let her own sadness taint their joy. "I'm thrilled for you both, Kellan."

"We're going to name him Trevor Buckley Blackwood," Kellan continued, his blue gaze growing serious. "In memory of all that Dad did for Irina."

Kellan excused himself while Miranda battled to get her emotions under control. She was so happy for Buckley's family. So why did she feel on the verge of tears?

Breathe in. Breathe out.

Standing off to one side of the raised platform where the podium had been stationed, Miranda focused on her breathing while the bandleader brought the song to a close. The partygoers clapped, and Miranda climbed the carpeted steps to take her place in front of the gala guests. Her small perch looked out over the dance floor, and to the rest of the great room beyond. The lighting was a dim violet, but she could still discern the faces in the gala, even as a spotlight snapped on over the podium.

"Good evening." She spoke into the microphone, pausing a moment to let the crowd take notice and tune in before she continued. Once more, she searched for Kai and didn't see him anywhere, his absence emphasizing the emptiness inside her.

Part of her short speech was just for him.

Swallowing hard, she told herself to forge ahead anyhow so she could go find him once she was done. Clearing her throat, she spoke into the microphone.

"Thank you all for being here at Royal Gives Back. I organized this benefit at the behest of Buckley Blackwood, a secret philanthropist who came to understand that all the millions he made during his lifetime couldn't compare to the joys of doing good for others." Her gaze traveled over her notes and then lifted to the attentive crowd. "And his wealth certainly couldn't compare to the rewards of his family."

The room seemed to go even more silent as if everyone gave her their full attention now, even the servers and musicians. Miranda bit her lip to keep her emotions in check, knowing the importance of giving Buckley a proper send-off. The weight of responsibility he'd given her settled on her shoulders one last time, and she hoped she proved worthy of his trust.

"Buckley found it hard to admit his mistakes in life. But before he died, he came to terms with the things he'd done wrong, and he chose to leave a legacy of philanthropy that we're celebrating to-

night. It's my pleasure to announce that every cent
we raise at Royal Gives Back will be matched by
Green Room Media, thanks to Nigel Townshend."
She waited while the assembled guests whooped and
applauded. The engineer working the lights searched
the crowd to find Nigel beside Sophie at a table in the
back, and the producer waved a good-natured hand.

Sophie beamed proudly beside him.

Miranda remembered her stepdaughter's advice
about Kai. *First, you apologize.* Then she'd worry
about the rest. All the more motivated to wind things
up so she could get to Deer Springs, Miranda read
the segment of her speech that was in memory of
Buckley's first wife, then talked briefly about how
the fundraising efforts would aid stroke research.

Then, Miranda tucked her notes to one side.

She was just about to conclude her remarks with
a personal addendum when she thought she heard
a stirring of movement at the back of the room. A
shuffle of feet. Low murmured voices.

Movement in the crowd alerted her to a dark-
haired man walking closer to the front of the podium.

Kai Maddox stopped in the middle of the dance
floor, separated from her by only a few couples in
black tie. Her heart pounded so hard she was sure the
microphone would pick it up and amplify it through
the venue. His green eyes gave away nothing. She
felt shaky as she started to speak again.

"Finally," she continued, pulling in a deep breath

and willing herself to get this part right. For Kai. "I am grateful to Buckley for giving me this opportunity to return to Royal. While I was as stunned as any of you at the initial terms of his will, I hope I have grown as a person over these last five months—" Her throat closed up. She had to pause for a moment. "And I'm so glad to feel like I have a family here. Now that Blackwood Bank and the other Blackwood assets are in the hands of their rightful heirs, I could officially head back to New York."

Her gaze locked on Kai's handsome face. The face of the man she loved more than she could have ever imagined possible.

"But overseeing Buckley's estate has taught me not to take for granted the time with family and loved ones. So I'm going to stay in Royal a little while longer to open a local Goddess fitness center." There was a murmur of surprise in the audience. Guests turned to one another. But Kai remained motionless, his face a mask. Miranda dug deep, pulling out the words that were meant for him alone. "Besides, I have unfinished business with a certain technology CEO who means the world to me. A man who—I hope—understands the value of a second chance."

He made his way across the room and the crowd began to part for Kai, his gaze locked on her with every purposeful stride. A spark of hope ignited inside her as she wondered if there could be a way forward for them after all. Maybe putting her heart out there for him to see could be enough. Perhaps he could hear the genuineness of her apology and her love.

Kai took the stairs two at a time to reach her. To tell her he wasn't ready to give her that chance? Or to tell her that he wanted to work things out with her, too? Uncertainty made her hands shake as she switched off the microphone and the crowd applauded.

When Kai swooped her up into his arms, the applause redoubled to become thunderous. Miranda looped her arms around his neck, holding tight. He hadn't spoken yet, but surely the action—his being here and holding her—meant something.

"I'm so sorry I doubted you," she told him, hoping against hope that he liked the idea of a second chance. "Kai, I want to do everything I can to make things work between us."

"In that case, we can't possibly fail." His strong arms flexed beneath her, lifting her a fraction so that his forehead tipped to hers while the band resumed playing nearby and the spotlight faded from the speaker's podium. "I happen to know you can move mountains if you set your mind to it, Miranda."

Closing her eyes, she gave herself a moment to soak in the feel of his arms tightened around her, the warmth of his forehead where it rested against hers. She breathed in the scent of his aftershave. Then, Kai straightened and carried her through the parted curtains that led to a small backstage area where extra tables and chairs were kept for events. He ignored the sign that said No Exit on a rear entrance and backed them through it, landing them in the parking area of the Texas Cattleman's Club, close to one of the side gardens.

Lowering Miranda to her feet, he took her hand and led her down a stone path to a secluded garden bench near a fountain.

"When I didn't see you earlier tonight, I was afraid you weren't coming. I planned to drive to Deer Springs right after I spoke so that I could apologize to you in person."

"I'm glad." Kai threaded her fingers through his, one by one as he let out a ragged sigh of relief. He pressed the back of her hand to his lips for a moment, his eyes sliding closed before he looked up again, his eyes open now and alive with desire. "Not that I needed the apology, but it makes me happy to hear you were making it a priority to talk to me. I know I haven't done a good job communicating what's important to me in the past, but I'm determined to do better with you in the future."

Hope sprang to life inside her, green and bright. He'd spoken exactly the kinds of words she'd longed to hear from him so many years ago.

"You're thinking about a future together, too?" she asked, turning more fully toward him on the bench so her knee bumped his.

He took her breath away in his tuxedo, his broad shoulders filling out the black silk and casting her in shadow as she gazed up at him. Music from the gala seeped through the walls and windows, a lively country tune that would have the whole crowd two-stepping in their tuxes and gowns.

"I'm doing more than thinking about it," Kai promised, his thumb rubbing over the back of her hand and making her shiver from the simple pleasure of it. "I'm going to do everything in my power to make sure the logistics of our relationship will work."

A relationship. Something lasting. He was meeting her halfway in this, the way a real relationship worked.

"I really do want to stay in Royal for a while," she assured him, eager to do her part, make their commitment a two-way street that would pay off so beautifully for both of them. She'd given a lot of thought to bringing a Goddess fitness center to town, and she knew it was the perfect way to spend more time cementing what she had with Kai. "I've been so happy here—except for the past week, of course. I've missed you every minute we weren't together."

"I've missed you, too. I knew I was missing the big picture, but it took Dane rattling my cage a little to make me see I was never going to be happy until I took a risk and laid my heart at your feet." He cupped her cheek with his free hand, stroking along her jaw. "Tonight, I'm doing just that. I love you, Miranda, so damn much."

Her heart soared. A smile curved her lips, relief and joy wrapping around her like a hug.

"Oh, Kai." Leaning into him, she kissed him gently, taking her time to feel the exquisite pleasure of this man's lips on hers, a pleasure she looked forward to revisiting as often as she wanted. "I love you, too. I regret that I didn't work harder to make things right between us the first time, but I'm not going to take what we have for granted ever again."

She'd meant every word of her speech at the podium. Seeing her first husband's mistakes up close and personal had helped her see that she would never be happy pursuing her business goals at the expense of everything else. She would make time for love in her life, even if it sometimes felt riskier than her career.

She trusted Kai with her heart.

When he eased back to look at her, his feelings were all right there for her to see. Full of love and a promise for the future.

"Maybe we both needed the time to grow and appreciate what we had to make it work this time," Kai reassured her, his words a soft whisper over her lips. He kissed her again with slow thoroughness that left her breathless. Then, he nipped her lower lip and backed away again. "But I promise you, we'll get it right now that we have this second chance."

"Even with you based in Deer Springs and my company in New York?" She didn't mind flying back and forth, but he'd said something about taking the logistics into account, and she was curious what that meant.

"Listen," he began, releasing her hand to cradle

her face between his palms. "I want you to take the deal with AMuse and follow all your dreams, Miranda. I can open a Madtec office in New York so we can have a life together there, too. We don't have to choose. We can have it all."

She believed him.

More than that, she believed in *them*.

Together, they could take on the world.

"I like the idea of sharing all our future plans." She remembered sitting in the Deer Springs Diner all those years ago, telling him about the life she'd imagined for herself. Listening to him spin lofty goals of his own. "We were always good at dreaming big."

"Now that we've established that we're sticking together forever, would you like to go back inside and dance with me?" Kai's green gaze tracked over her. "You look stunning tonight."

Her pulse quickened.

"Actually, I was already plotting my escape after my speech," she told him honestly. "I'd rather you take me home and make love to me all night long."

With a husky growl of approval, he drew her to her feet, a hand curving possessively around her waist, landing on the bare patch of skin where her dress had a cutout.

"I drove my motorcycle tonight. Can you manage the bike in that dress for a moonlight ride?"

"Are you kidding?" She began to walk backward toward the parking lot, tugging him with her. "I've been dying for an excuse to wrap my arms around you. Lead the way."

His teeth flashed white as he stepped ahead of her, guiding her through the parking area toward their future. It promised to be a wild and incredible ride.

Epilogue

One Week Later

"Do you, Lulu Shepard, take this man…"

Kai listened to the officiant's words at the wedding ceremony, but his eyes weren't on the bride as he stood under the huge white canopy erected near the pool at Blackwood Hollow for the televised nuptials of Lulu Shepard and Kace LeBlanc. Granted, the bride was a beauty in her simple white gown that showed off the natural beauty of her glossy black hair and almond-shaped brown eyes. But Kai's eyes kept straying to one of the lovely bridesmaids. He could manage only to glance over to the couple in question.

Miranda's costar from *Secret Lives of NYC Ex-*

Wives glowed, rushing to answer the question with an emphatic, "I do."

Her groom looked at her like he'd won the wife lottery.

Kai noted their happiness—and then returned his focus to the redheaded bridesmaid. Miranda stood with Lulu's other costars at the front of the canopy, the hem of her pale yellow bridesmaid's dress blowing gently around her legs thanks to the cooling fans placed around the tent for the sunset exchange of vows. She carried a small bouquet of purple violets. As always, Miranda captivated him.

She was everything he'd ever wanted in a woman—smart and ambitious, but tender and kind. She devoted herself to her charity and her loved ones even more than she committed herself to her work. Considering how far she'd come as a businesswoman, that was saying something. Kai's heart damned near burst with love for her as a quintet of musicians launched into a triumphant wedding recessional. Lulu and Kace led the way, holding their joined hands up in victory as a newly married pair, but Kai's attention stayed on Miranda where she walked through the aisle, each step bringing her closer to him.

The television cameras moved smoothly with the wedding party, tracking their every step while keeping out of the way. The ceremony was informal enough that the bride and groom were skipping a reception line since the party would start straight away. Photos had already been taken before the vows, so

Kai looked forward to Miranda being free for the rest of the evening.

Her blue eyes found his among the guests milling about to admire the wedding cake on a table at the back of the tent. A space for dancing was set up as a country band readied to take over for the chamber musicians now that the formal part of the evening was finished. Flashes popped on cell phones as guests all hurried to capture the bride and groom in their first moments of married life.

All of that activity around him was just a backdrop for his night with Miranda, the most important woman in the world to him.

He pulled her to him as soon as she reached him, indulging in a brief kiss to her cheek and neck, her jasmine scent an aphrodisiac after the tantalizing nights they'd spent together.

"Well, hello to you, too," Miranda murmured warmly, clutching his shoulder with one hand while she still held her bouquet with the other.

"Public displays of affection are allowed at a wedding, right?" He forced himself to step back a fraction, but he wound an arm around her waist, his fingers gliding along the pale yellow silk of her gown.

"Absolutely." Her smile lit her whole face as she gazed up at him. "It seems only appropriate to celebrate a new love match with a kiss."

She set down her flowers on a nearby folding chair.

"Would you like to step outside for a minute?" he suggested, nodding toward the pool area visible on the other end of the tent. "It's a beautiful night."

"Sounds good." She threaded her arm through his so he could escort her among the folding chairs to a spot where they could exit the canopy.

The spring Texas air was warmer, even with the sun going down and a breeze stirring. The landscape lights reflected in the pool and violet stars winked overhead in the fading twilight. Kai followed the smooth stone path behind the water feature. Here, trees arched over the path, their leaves fluttering softly.

The country band launched into its first tune, and a whoop went up inside the canopy.

"Are you sorry to see your show end for another season?" Kai asked as he twirled her under his arm in a silent invitation to dance.

Miranda fell into step with him easily, as if they'd been together for a lifetime. He still couldn't quite believe his good fortune finding her again after the past ten years apart. This time, nothing would come between them. He felt it with unswerving certainty.

"No." She shook her head, the red strands of her silky hair catching the moonlight. "The whole season has felt like a finale to me, not just the wedding episode. I've loved my time with the women on this show, but I think I'm ready to turn my attention to other things in the coming year."

He'd sensed the same thing in the way she'd talked

about the other cast members. With both Seraphina and Lulu getting married and moving to Texas, the group seemed to be moving on. He smoothed a hand up her spine and back down, savoring the feel of her. Grateful as hell to hold her in his arms.

"You know I'll stand behind whatever decision you make," he assured her. "But if I have my way, you won't be an 'ex-wife' for much longer."

He didn't want to rush Miranda, but he also knew that he wanted forever with this woman.

Her breath caught and she blinked twice before a smile curved her lips. "Something tells me it's going to be an exciting year."

Kai tipped her chin up with his knuckle, looking deep into her eyes.

"Have I told you today how much I love you?" He leaned in to kiss her and they swayed together, lips locked, for a long moment.

"No." Her eyes simmered with blue fire. "But I'm going to have you show me tonight instead."

With pleasure, Kai vowed to do just that.

* * * * *

Follow the drama in Royal, Texas,
with Texas Cattleman's Club: Rags to Riches!
It begins with
The Price Of Passion
by USA TODAY *bestselling author*
Maureen Child
Available June 2020!

#2737 THE PRICE OF PASSION

Texas Cattleman's Club: Rags to Riches • by Maureen Child

Rancher Camden Guthrie is back in Royal, Texas, looking to rebuild his life as a member of the Texas Cattleman's Club. The one person who can help him? Beth Wingate, his ex. Their reunion is red-hot, but startling revelations threaten their future.

#2738 FORBIDDEN LUST

Dynasties: Seven Sins • by Karen Booth

Allison Randall has long desired playboy Zane Patterson. The problem? He's her brother's best friend, and Zane won't betray that bond, no matter how much he wants her. Stranded in paradise, sparks fly, but Allison has a secret that could tear them apart...

#2739 UPSTAIRS DOWNSTAIRS TEMPTATION

The Men of Stone River • by Janice Maynard

Working in an isolated mansion, wealthy widower Farrell Stone needs a live-in housekeeper. Ivy Danby is desperate for a job to support her baby. Their simmering attraction for one another is evident, but are their differences too steep a hurdle to create a future together?

#2740 HOT NASHVILLE NIGHTS

Daughters of Country • by Sheri WhiteFeather

Brooding songwriter Spencer Riggs is ready to reinvent himself. His ex, Alice McKenzie, is the perfect stylist for the job. Years after their wild and passionate romance, Alice finally has her life on track, but will their sizzling attraction burn them both again?

#2741 SCANDALOUS ENGAGEMENT

Lockwood Lightning • by Jules Bennett

To protect her from a relentless ex, restauranteur Reese Conrad proposes to his best friend, Josie Coleman. But their fake engagement reveals real feelings, and Josie sees Reese in a whole new way. And just as things heat up, a shocking revelation changes everything!

#2742 BACK IN HIS EX'S BED

Murphy International • by Joss Wood

Art historian Finn Murphy has a wild, impulsive side. It's what his ex-wife, Beah Jenkinson, found so attractive—and what burned down their white-hot marriage. Now, reunited to plan a friend's wedding, the chemistry is still there... and so are the problems that broke them apart.

SPECIAL EXCERPT FROM

⬧HARLEQUIN
DESIRE

*To protect her from a relentless ex, restaurateur Reese
Conrad proposes to his best friend, Josie Coleman.
But their fake engagement reveals real feelings, and
Josie sees Reese in a whole new way. And just as things
heat up, a shocking revelation changes everything!*

Read on for a sneak peek at
Scandalous Engagement
by USA TODAY *bestselling author Jules Bennett.*

"What's that smile for?" he asked.

She circled the island and placed a hand over his heart. "You're
just remarkable. I mean, I've always known, but lately you're just
proving yourself more and more."

He released the wine bottle and covered her hand with his...and
that's when she remembered the kiss. She shouldn't have touched
him—she should've kept her distance because there was that look
in his eyes again. Where had this come from? When did he start
looking at her like he wanted to rip her clothes off and have his
naughty way with her?

"We need to talk about it," he murmured.

It. As if saying the word *kiss* would somehow make this situation
weirder. And as if she hadn't thought of anything else since *it* had
happened.

"Nothing to talk about," she told him, trying to ignore the warmth
and strength between his hand and his chest.

"You can't say you weren't affected."

"I didn't say that."

He tipped his head, somehow making that penetrating stare even
more potent. "It felt like more than a friend kiss."

Way to state the obvious.

"And more than just a practice," he added.

HDEXP0520

Josie's heart kicked up. They were too close, talking about things that were too intimate. No matter what she felt, what she thought she wanted, this wasn't right. She couldn't ache for her best friend in such a physical way. If that kiss changed things, she couldn't imagine how anything more would affect this relationship.

"We can't go there again," she told him. "I mean, you're a good kisser—"

"Good? That kiss was a hell of a lot better than just good."

She smiled. "Fine. It was pretty incredible. Still, we can't get caught up in this whole fake-engagement thing and lose sight of who we really are."

His free hand came up and brushed her hair away from her face. "I haven't lost sight of anything. And I'm well aware of who we are…and what I want."

Why did that sound so menacing in the most delicious of ways? Why was her body tingling so much from such simple touches when she'd firmly told herself to not get carried away?

Wait. Was he leaning in closer?

"Reese, what are you doing?" she whispered.

"Testing a theory."

His mouth grazed hers like a feather. Her knees literally weakened as she leaned against him for support. Reese continued to hold her hand against his chest, but he wrapped the other arm around her waist, urging her closer.

There was no denying the sizzle or spark or whatever the hell was vibrating between them. She'd always thought those cheesy expressions were so silly, but there was no perfect way to describe such an experience.

And kissing her best friend was quite an experience…

Don't miss what happens next in…
Scandalous Engagement
by USA TODAY *bestselling author Jules Bennett.*

Available June 2020 wherever
Harlequin Desire books and ebooks are sold.

Harlequin.com

Get 4 FREE REWARDS!

We'll send you 2 FREE Books plus 2 FREE Mystery Gifts.

Harlequin Desire® books transport you to the world of the American elite with juicy plot twists, delicious sensuality and intriguing scandal.

FREE Value Over **$20**

YES! Please send me 2 FREE Harlequin Desire novels and my 2 FREE gifts (gifts are worth about $10 retail). After receiving them, if I don't wish to receive any more books, I can return the shipping statement marked "cancel." If I don't cancel, I will receive 6 brand-new novels every month and be billed just $4.55 per book in the U.S. or $5.24 per book in Canada. That's a savings of at least 13% off the cover price! It's quite a bargain! Shipping and handling is just 50¢ per book in the U.S. and $1.25 per book in Canada.* I understand that accepting the 2 free books and gifts places me under no obligation to buy anything. I can always return a shipment and cancel at any time. The free books and gifts are mine to keep no matter what I decide.

225/326 HDN GNND

Name (please print)

Address   Apt. #

City   State/Province   Zip/Postal Code

Mail to the **Reader Service:**
IN U.S.A.: P.O. Box 1341, Buffalo, NY 14240-8531
IN CANADA: P.O. Box 603, Fort Erie, Ontario L2A 5X3

Want to try 2 free books from another series? Call 1-800-873-8635 or visit www.ReaderService.com.

IF YOU ENJOYED THIS BOOK
WE THINK YOU WILL ALSO LOVE

✦ HARLEQUIN
PRESENTS

Escape to exotic locations where passion knows no bounds.

Welcome to the glamorous lives of royals and billionaires, where passion knows no bounds. Be swept into a world of luxury, wealth and exotic locations.

8 NEW BOOKS AVAILABLE EVERY MONTH!

Love Harlequin romance?

DISCOVER.

Be the first to find out about promotions, news and exclusive content!

Facebook.com/HarlequinBooks

Twitter.com/HarlequinBooks

Instagram.com/HarlequinBooks

Pinterest.com/HarlequinBooks

ReaderService.com

EXPLORE.

Sign up for the Harlequin e-newsletter and download a free book from any series at **TryHarlequin.com**

CONNECT.

Join our Harlequin community to share your thoughts and connect with other romance readers!
Facebook.com/groups/HarlequinConnection

HARLEQUIN